THE END UNSEEN

EVEN ANGELS CANNOT ESCAPE TRAGEDY

ARIEL N. ANDERSON

Cover Design by Ria Raven Graphic Design

Graphic Design by Inda Ashes Art

Character Artwork by Rilee Harris

eBook ISBN: 979-8-9987836-6-1

Paperback ISBN: 979-8-9987836-7-8

Hardcover ISBN: 979-8-9987836-8-5

First Edition: April 2026

10 9 8 7 6 5 4 3 2 1

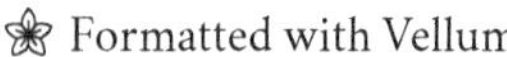 Formatted with Vellum

PROCEED
WITH CAUTION

This book has a tragic ending. Please tread carefully.

Other Content Warnings Include: violence, sex, misogyny, immigration and asylum, welfare, death of a child (baby), xenophobia, and war.

This book does not include graphic sexual content, but the themes inside are intended for mature audiences only.

Questions regarding the content of this book can be directed to author@arielandersonauthor.com

National Suicide Prevention Lifeline:
1-800-273-8255

A small portion of the net royalties from all Ariel N. Anderson titles are donated to the American Foundation for Suicide Prevention

To those who are suffering from wars that are not yours.

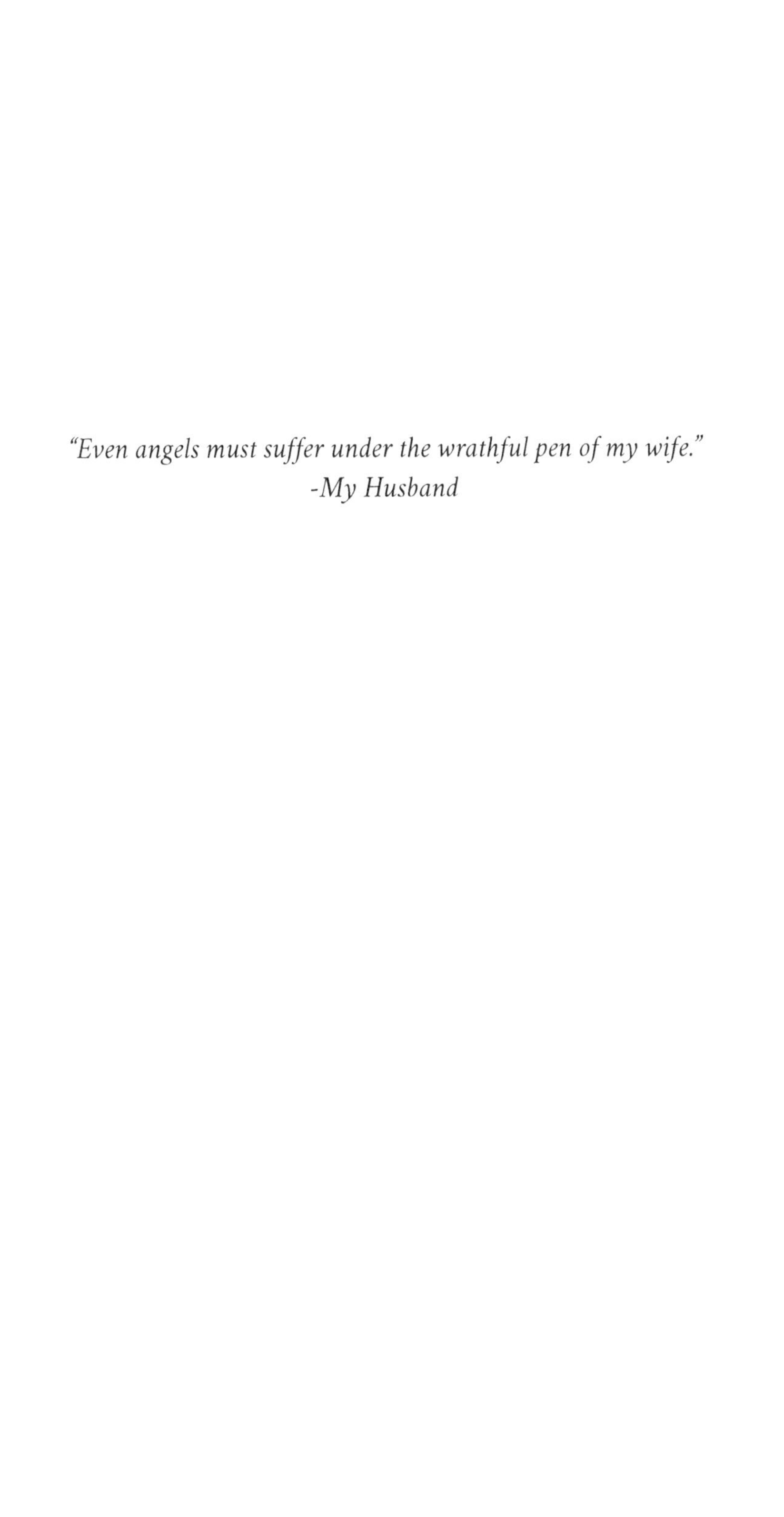

"*Even angels must suffer under the wrathful pen of my wife.*"
-*My Husband*

PLAYLIST

The Sons of Sanguinius - Edwin Montgomery
The Sound of Silence - Disturbed
God Help the Outcasts - Sierra Nelson
Zombie - Bad Wolves
21 Guns (feat. The Cast of American Idiot) - Green Day
War Lord - 2WEI
Angels Fall - Breaking Benjamin
Lift Me Up - Rihanna

PROLOGUE

The night had long since turned still, but sleep refused him. Val-Theris stood in the upper observatory, surrounded by the faint rustling of maps catching on the wind, and the cold breath of open air. Beneath the glass dome, Solmiris glittered like a field of gold stretched to the horizon and carved into the cliffside.

It should have comforted him.

Instead, it felt fragile. Too bright. Too temporary.

Tonight, a dull ache clutched the base of his skull, and the lights of the city below began to bleed into one another. He had learned to sense when a vision was coming, but they always seemed to crash into him like a tide when he wanted them least.

He pressed both palms to the marble railing of the balcony, and the world folded inwards. The chamber dissolved into light. The air thickened with the scent of dust and rain and ruin.

He stood before a statue of a woman, serene and sorrowful, with a baby in her arms.

She rose twice his height, carved from marble so white it glowed faintly even in shadow. Every line of her face was grace itself, etched with the quiet strength of a mother and the pain of loss. Her expression seemed carved from mercy, and there was a single tear streaking down her cheek.

Behind her, the Golden City lay in ruin.

The towers cracked. The great dome of the palace had fallen in two. Gold leaf peeled from the walls like burned skin. The air was full of dust and the faint echo of weeping.

Val-Theris reached out to touch the statue's face, somehow growing more distorted the more he studied it.

"Who are you?" he whispered. "Why do you weep?"

The child in the statue's arms was faceless, too. He tried to look closer, but the more he strained, the blurrier the features became.

He reached out to caress the infant's face, but the marble fractured under his touch. Val-Theris stumbled back, clutching his temples as the vision rushed through him: the city collapsing, fire covering the land, men, women, and children sobbing in the streets.

And in the distance, Val-Theris saw a glimpse of himself. His unmistakable feathered wings sat atop his throne, watching it all.

When he came back to himself, he was on his knees in the observatory, his breath ragged, his hands slick with blood from his nose. The city below gleamed and he stared out over it, trembling.

The statue's face lingered behind his eyelids as he rose slowly and turned his gaze toward the distant horizon where Lunareth and Korvath slept under flickering stars.

WHEN VAL-THERIS DESCENDED the upper district to the lower plaza, the wind carried the scent of morning dew. The sun had not yet broken the horizon and the stone beneath his boots gleamed pale and colorless.

In the center of the plaza, there was no statue, of course. Only a blank pedestal veined with cracks and moss, standing lonely in the center of the wide court.

But Val-Theris felt it. The echo of it. Every inch of air seemed heavy with the memory of something he had yet to lose. He stood motionless, wings drawn close, eyes fixed on the emptiness before him.

Rohannes lingered a few paces back, silent as his shadow. He had learned not to speak when the visions left their mark on the king like this.

Val-Theris's hand tightened on the hilt at his side. "It was here," he murmured.

The Angelicus Prime tilted his head. "My lord?"

"The woman and the child made of stone. She stood right here."

Rohannes said nothing, for he did not know what to say. The king rarely shared his visions, and never with anyone other than him. He had heard fragments before, of course, sometimes finding his king half-dazed with blood pooling on his upper lip from his nose. But he had never seen his king so still, so stripped of the armor of command and crown.

The silence stretched long enough for the wind to shift and the sun to rise, carrying a distant clamor from the gates. Val-Theris's feathers flared in reflex. The Angelicus Prime took his leave to address the commotion while the king stood silent. When Rohannes returned, he brought news.

"There are travelers at the gates. Maybe a hundred or so. They bear no banners, and claim to be refugees from Lunareth, begging sanctuary within our walls."

Val-Theris, for a long moment, said nothing. Then, quietly, "Open the gates."

THE ROAD to the lower terraces overflowed with movement. The first of the refugees had barely crossed the gates, yet the air already thrummed with noise and dust.

Val-Theris stood above it all in the plaza, unmoved from before, flanked only by Rohannes and two silent sentinels. From here he could see the mass of weary travelers: women carrying what little they could salvage, children too tired even to cry.

Very few men, he noticed, came with them. What men there were had either seen too many winters, or too few to even call them men.

A sudden break in the crowd drew his gaze. A young woman had stopped at the base of the hill, helping an older woman to her feet. She straightened slowly, brushing dust from the skirt of her dress. The morning light spilled over her dark hair and sun-kissed skin, catching in the folds of her shawl, turning the edges to silver.

For one breathless instant, from where Val-Theris stood, she aligned perfectly with the broken pedestal in the center of the plaza.

It was as though she were standing *on it.*

The sun struck her profile. Around her, the golden walls gleamed like the remnants of his vision. He felt that strange tightening in his chest. Rohannes said something, but Val-Theris didn't hear it. His eyes were fixed on the woman below.

His voice faltered, speaking quietly into the wind. *"Is this why you weep?"*

The woman lifted her head just then, as if she had heard him, or some invisible string lifted her soft green gaze for her. Their eyes met across the distance, too brief to mean anything at all, but something passed between them all the same:

The soft shock of inevitability.

The girl blinked, her hand rising instinctively to her chest. Val-Theris felt his own do the same, and then exhaled a shaky breath. The ache of her gaze lodged itself into his ribs like a shard of glass. Then the crowd shifted, swallowing her from view.

When he finally spoke, his voice was thin. "I want their leaders brought before me as soon as they settle."

Rohannes inclined his head, still oblivious to the tremor in his king's tone.

Val-Theris turned from the pedestal, but as he returned to his golden throne, his skull throbbed with the effort of trying to remember if the features in the marble were that of the Lunarethian girl.

ONE

THE RIVER DIDN'T JUST CARRY freshwater, it carried the music of Lunareth.

From the winding terraces carved into the sandstone cliffs, the soft hum of woven drums mingled with the bright trill of reed flutes carried on the warm breeze down into the valley below. The lanterns had been strung early for the Festival of First Light, their pale silks and paper suns swaying gently in the twilight, painting the narrow streets in rippling shades of gold, indigo, and silver.

Jesenia stood barefoot on the smooth clay steps outside her family's stone home, her shawl loose about her shoulders, its silver-threaded hem glinting faintly beneath the soft glow of hanging lamps. It had belonged to her beloved grandmother, who raised her and her brother.

In her country, family heirlooms were more valuable than gold, and so she was never seen without it. If it wasn't hanging on her shoulders, it was draped over her hair and tied under her chin on a hot day.

Children raced past her, their laughter ringing sharp and

bright as they scattered into the growing crowd gathered near the marketplace. Merchants called over one another from their stalls, voices lilting and rich, offering dyed silks, bowls of saffroned rice, carved ivory beads, and cups of chilled persimmon wine.

Lunareth was more alive under the moon, and Jesenia lifted her chin to breathe in a deep inhale of the cool night air.

She felt a poke at her back and lightly squealed, turning to find the smiling face of her older brother, Danyel, behind her with his arms crossed loosely over his chest, painted in intricate patterns for the festival.

"You're being strangely quiet," he jested, softly nudging her shoulder, but they both knew Jesenia had never been a girl with many words, even before their grandmother had died. "Come to the square. Dance. Eat. Live."

"Danyel–" Jesenia started, but he cut her off.

"No. No talk of the whispers you hear of war. Not tonight."

"If not tonight, then when? We dance in the moonlight as Korvath marches towards our hills."

"You don't know that, Jesenia!" Danyel said, louder than he meant to. He took a deep breath and gave his sister a stern look. "Seraveth is a country far richer in resources than Lunareth. If war is coming, it's heading for the Golden City." Danyel took her arm and pulled her close before patting her dark hair with his hand. "We will be fine."

Jesenia gave him a soft smile. "I hope you are right."

"When have I ever been wrong?" he asked with a grin, returning to the crowd and disappearing behind a group of dancers.

Jesenia visited a stall for a warm tea before returning to the steps of her home. She took a seat there and watched as the people began to gather near the river bank.

The town elders in flowing robes knelt at the edge, whispering blessings as the children eagerly lined up in front of them to leave offerings of seeds and flower petals. Once the paper lantern was filled with the gifts, the elders set it alight and gently pushed it into the river. The soft golden glow drifted lazily along the current until it disappeared into the night.

Jesenia, for a fleeting moment, wondered if the river would still carry the lantern next year.

The drums deepened, the voices of her people rising in song as hundreds of lanterns drifted out beneath the silvery banners strung between the terraces.

From above, Lunareth shimmered like a constellation carved into earth and stone, its colors alive, its people's laughter folding soft into the hum of the river. Jesenia quietly watched the remainder of the festival from afar until the lanterns burned themselves out and her people began to slowly return to their homes.

Festival dancers passed, their silk sleeves embroidered with bright colors and their wrists and ankles adorned with heavy bangles.

The Lunarethians prized artistry above all else, surviving by selling little trinkets and colorful dresses to passing merchants, who went on to sell them in the larger cities as novelties.

The walls of the stone cottages were adorned with mosaics of their ancestor's myths, of the river, of musicians and dancers. The murals lined the cobbled streets, and the Lunarethians knew that their people kept their homes open to each other.

Jesenia was proud of her people and the way they relived their history and honored their grief through beauty.

Tragedy was rare in Jesenia's country. Her people kept out of the wars and politics of the larger realms, but her village was directly between the bloodthirsty rule of Korvath and the opulent riches of Seraveth, so she worried that war would come for them, *eventually*.

JESENIA WOKE to the sound of screaming.

She shot up from her small bed, meeting her brother's eyes. He gave her a concerned look, then went outside to see what was happening. Jesenia waited with bated breath, her palms sweating through her thin blanket.

Something in the air shifted. There was a fracture in time that made her stomach drop, followed by a hush so sudden it unsettled her bones under her skin.

Then there was chaos. It was no longer one woman screaming. It was women, children, men. The noise was louder, closer. Jesenia watched as a single flaming arrow crashed through the glass of her window, setting alight a wooden shelf of books in the room before spreading to the kitchen.

Jesenia froze, unable to comprehend what was happening as she watched fire take her home bit by bit.

Danyel crashed through the door, seizing Jesenia's wrist and shouting at her, but she couldn't hear him. He gathered what little he could grab into his arms and dragged her out of the house.

What Jesenia saw outside was the embodiment of Hell. The crowd splintered in different directions. Children were abandoned in the streets. Merchant stalls were already burned to the ground. Jesenia finally came to her senses, grabbing the two lonely children, one in each hand, and followed her brother. To where? She didn't know. She wasn't even sure what was happening, but Danyel was running, and so she ran with him.

Jesenia stumbled over debris as she ran through the fire-lined streets.

Fire. That was all she could see. It was all she could hear—crackling, swallowing wood and silk and the painted stones of her people's homes. Everything was now painted in flames or soot.

And then she finally saw the harbingers of this disaster.

Out of the flames and the shadows spilled soldiers armored in black steel, their long, precise blades catching the reddish-orange glow of the fire. They laughed as they murdered Jesenia's people in the streets. Laughed as children cried at their mother's corpse. Laughed as they dragged women by their ankles across the dirt, clawing away to try and escape their evil.

One of them met eyes with Jesenia, and he smiled, his teeth thick with blood. He was larger than the others, and wore a cape as black as his armor, and was drenched in malice. The fire seemed to warp around him. He dropped his sword and came for her and the children. She pushed their small, crying bodies behind her own and stood with her chin held high. He would not touch them without going through her.

Her voice broke, sharp, ragged. "Please. They're just children—"

"Jesenia, run!" Danyel yelled, his voice cracking against the roar of the crowd and the fire. He tackled the single soldier headed for Jesenia, but Danyel's frame was no match for the unflinching steel of his armor.

Danyel fell to the ground, disoriented and bleeding from a gash in his head. Jesenia cried, but could do nothing as she watched the soldier crack his relentless fist across her brother's bleeding face.

Danyel went limp, and Jesenia nearly fell to her knees, but another body caught her before she hit the ground. One of the village elders dragged her and the two children along with him by their clothes.

The soldier gave Jesenia one last smile before disappearing into the flames, but she finally heard him speak:

"For Korvath! Bow or burn!"

Something deep in her chest splintered at her brother's corpse, but her body moved anyway, pulling the two children through alleys as flame and steel roared around her.

The fire spread faster than she thought possible. The wind carried it along the rows of silks, across the shallow bridges, through the climbing terraces carved into the stone. One by one, the paper lanterns Jesenia had watched float so gently upon the river earlier burst into flame, their golden light swallowed beneath the smoke.

She thought of her people's mosaics, their river songs, their carved ancestral stones. She thought of the hundreds of lanterns she'd watched float into the darkness only hours ago, carrying wishes she'd whispered beneath her breath.

And for the first time in her life, Jesenia knew they wouldn't come true.

By dawn, the fires still smoldered. The people of Lunareth gathered on the northern road, carrying what little remained of their lives in woven baskets, bundled silks, and small wrapped satchels. Children clung to their mothers' skirts, their wide eyes fixed on the mountains ahead.

And Jesenia stood among them with her shawl drawn tightly around her shoulders, as the first rays of the sun touched the ash-streaked ruins of her city.

TWO

Though the fires of her home had vanished behind them two nights ago, the smell of smoke and suffering still clung to Jesenia's shawl. The silver-threaded hem was dulled with soot and dirt.

Before her, the road to the Golden City of Solmiris stretched endlessly beneath a gloom-filled sky. She looked upward, praying to the skies in hopes that it did not rain on her people and wash away the remainder of their fragile hope.

There were so few of them left. She hadn't counted, but Jesenia thought it couldn't be more than one hundred of them that had made it out. Most of them were women and small children, and they walked in silence. A line of sorrowful figures carrying nothing but the clothes on their backs.

There was no song now. No festival drums. No smell of saffron and jasmine on the wind.

Jesenia walked last, trailing behind the uneven line of weary bodies to make sure none of the children or elderly were left behind. Her thin sandals had worn through at the heel, and her feet were aching with each painful step, but she didn't let herself slow.

In front of her, a small boy's trembling legs finally gave out, and he stumbled as he clutched the hem of his grandmother's skirt. The woman looked dreadful, knowing she was in no state to carry the boy, so Jesenia knelt beside them.

"Come, little one," she murmured softly to the boy, scooping him into her already tired arms. His cheek pressed into her shoulder and his breath was shallow against her neck. "Just a little farther, hm?"

He didn't answer, already half asleep and his weight slack against Jesenia's weak body.

The old woman choked back a sob. "Blessings to you, girl."

Jesenia kept walking, not acknowledging the woman. She was close to breaking herself and didn't want anyone to see her cry. Her people were broken, hungry, and exhausted in ways she had never seen before.

Many of them still had open wounds and untreated burns from Korvath's raid. They had lost twenty people already on the road who succumbed to their injuries, and others looked like they might drop at any moment.

The Lunarethians had always been pacifists, careful to avoid conflict and war. Jesenia's people simply didn't believe in violence, even out of defense, and that was surely why there were so few of them left.

By midday on the third day, the hills began to rise. Soft slopes unfurled into ridges dotted with wildflowers and freshwater lakes. Beyond it all, Jesenia caught her first glimpse of the Golden City of Solmiris.

It almost didn't look real. Built high up into the cliffside, the walls of white stone protected the largest city any of the Lunarethians had ever seen. Golden spires, gilded cathedrals, and at the very top of the cliff, at the highest point in the city, a beautiful domed citadel sat overlooking the streets below.

It was so bright. So clean. So untouched. So perfect.

Around her, murmurs of hope and relief spread between dry, cracked lips.

The boy in her arms shifted. "What if the gates don't open?" he asked, his voice hoarse.

Jesenia smoothed his hair. "Oh, don't say such things. Of course they will open."

Though she cooed the reassurance to the boy, Jesenia wasn't sure she believed it herself. Just because the city was beautiful and wealthy didn't mean that her people would be welcomed.

But if they did not open the gates…they would have nowhere else to go.

Only when they were close enough to speak to the guardsmen at the gates did her people slow. Silence settled thick over them, laced with exhaustion, fear and fragile hope.

The gates themselves were taller than any story dared to tell. Pale stone veined with gold, each door etched with feathered wings so intricate they needed only a strong gust to take flight. The gates protected a city of silk, gold, and marble untouched by the ruin that pushed the Lunarethians there.

At the front of the group, one of the elders rasped to the sky. "Please. We have been forced from our homes. We are wounded and sick. We have children that have not eaten in days. I beg for the mercy of the great Angel-King."

The guards atop the wall stood unmoving, halberds upright, their gold-etched, crimson-plumed helms glinting in the sunlight.

"Solmiris's walls do not open for *foreigners*."

The disdain in his voice made Jesenia cower. It was true that the capital cities of Korvath and Seraveth were not known for allowing outsiders within their walls, but could they not see how desperate Jesenia's people were? How the elders had dropped to their knees to beg for a small mercy?

"Please," Jesenia whispered, a single tear falling from her eye. Her silver-threaded shawl was caught between her fingers as she looked at the men atop the walls.

The sun climbed higher, hot and burning against the backs of weary necks. More soldiers had come to stare, joined even by a few citizens. Beside Jesenia, a young mother cried when she tried to feed her infant only to find she had no milk left to give.

Suddenly, she felt a shift in the air, and the whispers of the guards grew into shouts. Jesenia felt the earth rumble beneath her feet. With a grinding of marble and steel, Solmiris's gates slowly parted. Jesenia's people rushed to their feet, filtering into the relief behind walls. Bodies pressed close and begged the guards they passed for water and bread.

Jesenia helped the grandmother and the child to their feet, entering the city behind the rest of her people. When she stepped through the gates and joined her people in the plaza, her eyes were pulled upward, where a god-like figure watched over the scene with careful eyes.

Val-Theris Angelicus, the Angel-King of Seraveth.

He was more handsome than any man could ever dare to be. Silky blonde hair touched his shoulders, and his piercing blue eyes swept over the crowd carefully. His body was adorned with fine golden armor that gleamed where the sun struck the plates. He was taller than the soldiers at his side, towering over them in both height and his commanding presence.

But it was the wings that caught her attention the most. Pale and vast and beautiful, the feathers were outstretched and shimmered as if veined with gold like everything else in the city.

She imagined he would look arrogant or cold, or would radiate fury and power to explain why whole legions of mortal men would die for him, for his throne. But he looked like none of those terrible things. There was the permanent downturn of the corners of his lips that did not belong on a face that appeared so young. There were shadows beneath his eyes where ruling had worn down the thin skin there.

A single moment passed where their gazes collided. He looked as though he was searching for something, and Jesenia could not make herself small enough to vanish under the weight of his attention.

Her hand lifted absently to her chest. She had heard stories, of course, of his grandeur, but only now could she see why they called him an angel.

Jesenia was forced to move along by the guards, and when she looked back up to where the king was standing, she only saw a glimpse of his wings as he turned away.

Her eyes and thoughts drifted away from him, taking in the rest of the lower ring of Solmiris. It stretched like a vision— cobblestone streets lined with carved fountains, silk banners rippling softly in the wind, well-kept homes adorned with cascades of flowers, ivy, and well-trimmed bushes. The splendor almost hurt to look at.

Jesenia's people were quickly ushered into a corner of the lower ring by the guards. The gates of Solmiris were hastily shut behind them, sealing them inside a city that clearly did not want them there. The guards looked at her and her people like a sickness, a poison, despite the many words of blessings and thanks for allowing her people inside.

She knew the relief here would be short-lived, but she could not dwell on it, for her throat was too dry and her stomach too empty.

The Elders were called to meet with the King in his citadel, and were given a single ear of raw corn to eat on their way to answer their summons.

The rest of Jesenia's people were given scraps meant for the pigs.

THREE

The throne room of Solmiris was a cathedral of gold and glass. The afternoon light poured through its high windows, painting fractured halos across the marble floor. Val-Theris sat upon the lower steps leading to his dais, wings folded tight behind him. His golden crown rested on his throne like a shackle he had discarded.

Val-Theris did not wear his crown, nor did he sit on his throne. He saw such things as indulgences, as vanity.

A crown and a throne make not a ruler, he always told those who asked why he chose to stand with his people, not above them.

Before him, five Lunarethian elders knelt. Their robes still smelled faintly of the smoke they left behind, and their eyes were hollow as they spoke.

"It was Korvath," said the one in the center, her voice rasping. "They took our food, stole away our women, slaughtered our families…" her voice trembled as tears slipped from her eyes, "and what they could not take, they burned."

The king leaned forward slightly, listening. He did not interrupt as every word settled in his chest like stone.

Another elder, his body aching with age, added, "We beg for sanctuary, O Great Val-Theris Angelicus, he who was born of his God's Light. We have nothing worthy of your favor, and only hope you will grace us with your mercy."

Val-Theris was quiet for a moment. "Solmiris will not turn away the lost," he said at last, his voice quiet but strong. The elders wept openly, one of them reaching to kiss the top of his boot. He gently stopped them with a hand. "Stand," he said, "There is no need for worship. Mercy is not my gift, it is my duty."

A slow clap echoed through the chamber from above.

"*Mercy is not my gift, it is my duty,*" mocked a voice from the upper balcony overlooking the throne. "How poetic, brother."

Val-Theris's spine stiffened. Val-Oros floated down, his armor black as night where his brother's gleamed gold. His smile was lazy and cruel, and the air seemed to darken around him, despite his flaming wings producing their own light.

Where Val-Theris was a soft radiance, Val-Oros was a living flame, and every soul in the room felt it.

"You should not be here," Val-Theris said evenly. "I did not invite you into these halls."

"And yet here I stand," Val-Oros replied, stroking his beard. "I find myself endlessly intrigued by your benevolence toward foreign scum."

"It is your insatiable violence that drove them here, brother."

The Bloodletter of Korvath stopped beside one of the Lunarethian elders, his hand harshly gripping the man's shoulder. The elder flinched. At the touch, Val-Oros's eyes turned white, burning with that cursed flicker of foresight.

He huffed out a scoff, turning his gaze toward Val-Theris. "I wouldn't waste the grain, this one will die soon enough."

Gasps rippled through the hall as the elder stumbled back, horror-struck. Val-Theris stepped toward his brother, putting space between him and the elders. His wings unfolded like blades of light in defense. "Enough."

They stood eye to eye, golden light against raging fire.

"You sit here among mortals and call it grace, but your compassion will break you sooner or later."

"Brother," Val-Theris said strongly, "you shame yourself in these halls. You drove these people here with your reckless fire, then possess the audacity to insult them for seeking refuge with me."

For a heartbeat, the entire chamber stood silent.

Val-Oros finally laughed. "You will learn, in time," he said to his brother before turning, his burning wings flaring once before he vanished through the arched doors.

When he was gone, Val-Theris lowered himself back onto his seat on the steps, the elders still trembling before him.

"Go," he said softly. "You are safe here."

They obeyed wordlessly, bowing deep at the waist as they left. The throne room emptied, leaving only Val-Theris with Rohannes at his side.

"I await the day you give the order to cut out that warmonger's tongue."

Val-Theris huffed out a humorless laugh as his gaze lingered on the doors. "He cannot help what he is," he murmured. "Our father made us twin vessels of the same curse. I chose light, he chose darkness. That is the only difference, Rohannes."

Val-Theris stood in the Hall of Radiance, where murals of all history stretched from marble floor to gilded ceiling. At the very center, carved into the wall itself, was the First Light, Val-Or, the mythical God who tore himself apart to bring two sons into the world.

The Angel-King raised his hand to the mural, his fingers tracing the faint cracks that had begun to web across the god's face. But Val-Theris had never seen him as a god. He called him something simpler: *father.*

In the beginning, there had only been one kingdom that worshipped Val-Or and served his divine throne. When the god's light and influence began to dull with time, he divided himself to give the people something real to follow. Half of him went to mercy and half of him went to might, shaping His perfect sons from each.

What the stories have forgotten through time, though, is that Val-Oros was the favored son. Their father was so careful in forming the herald of flame, and Val-Theris was meant to rule at his side, tempering the fire. Both brothers were given the gift of prophecy. Val-Theris could see the future in faceless fragments, and Val-Oros saw destiny only when it led to destruction.

They came to the world as young men, young gods, radiant and fierce. But jealousy grew quickly; Val-Oros was meant to be the new ruler of this world, but his mighty flame scorched the earth where his brother's light sowed reverence among the people. Many of them quickly learned to follow Val-Theris's radiance, and Val-Oros grew angry and scorned with time.

Eventually, the brothers grew apart, plagued by infighting between them. They parted ways, and Val-Theris raised the Kingdom of Seraveth, a luscious city of gold, law, and mercy. Val-Oros carved Korvath into the earth, the realm of flame and fear where obedience was sanctified by bloodshed. He dropped his father's name, and became known as Oros the Bloodletter, Oros the Warmonger.

In between their two kingdoms came Lunareth, city of the

night, built slowly by those who did not believe in wars or kings or gods.

The two brothers had not spoken face to face in years before today, and still, Val-Theris could feel the shadow of Korvath lingering long after its king left.

Val-Theris sank to one knee before the mural. "Why, father?" he whispered, his voice trembling with exhaustion more than sadness. "You made me a god, but gave me the heart of a man. You gave me sight enough to see suffering, but never enough strength to change it. You do not answer my prayers. Do you even watch over me?"

The mural said nothing back.

It never did.

FOUR

The rain had been falling since dawn, cold and harsh. The streets were nearly empty, at least in the upper districts where Solmiris's people had homes to hide in while the rain soaked the makeshift tents of the Lunarethian refugees.

Jesenia moved quickly and quietly, her foreign-dark hair hidden beneath her shawl as if her clothes did not immediately scream that she did not belong. The weight of that truth pressed heavy on her shoulders with every step through the clean stone streets and every step past the intricate glasswork windows.

She knew she shouldn't wander far from the quarter where her people now lived, but she had given her thin rations to a sick child, and the consequence of a painful belly forced her to look for scraps dumped in the back alleys before the rats got to them.

There were rumors that their rations would be cut off entirely. It had been only days, and the people of Solmiris already wanted the Lunarethians off their streets. So Jesenia walked, hoping to find something of sustenance for herself and her people.

The only thing she found was a man drinking outside a

tavern, promising her a bed tonight if only she'd share it *with* him. When she turned away from him, he threw the remainder of his pint against her backside, drenching her already soaked-through dress with his yeasty drink.

There was a sound approaching her, of boots on the rain-covered stone streets. The low murmur of voices grew louder, and Jesenia peaked around a corner, only to be thrust back harshly into a wall by a guard.

"Make way!" he shouted at her. A procession of guards filtered into the streets, and that's when she saw him.

Val-Theris walked in the center of his guard. He wore no helm to shield him from the rain, and so his golden hair clung to his skull as he marched with them. His wings shook occasionally to rid the feathers of the excess water.

Though she had already seen him once before, his splendor drew the eye the way the moon pulled the tides.

Jesenia could not will herself to look away, and as if some invisible thread tightened between them, his head turned. Not toward her, not fully at least. It was simply a shift in his attention as if something caught the corner of his vision, like instinct rather than choice.

The distance and bodies between them should have made it impossible for him to see her, and still, he somehow did. Her pulse stumbled when their eyes met for a moment longer than what could be considered a passing gaze. As if he somehow recognized her face among the dozens of strangers in his city.

Some member of his group grabbed his attention for a moment, and when the conversation ceased, his eyes found hers again—this time, too easily to be considered an accident.

But she told herself that the Angel-King had far greater burdens to bear than noticing a refugee in a dripping hood that wandered too far from her people.

Jesenia returned to the refugee quarter soon after, her belly partially full with half an apple and a soggy piece of bread.

As though it had been waiting for her, the shouting started almost as soon as she returned to her tent. It was sharp, uneven, desperate, and turned the attention of everyone who could hear it.

"They've cut us off! Three weeks without grain! Punishment for drinking from their wells! Fines for sleeping in their streets!"

A ripple of response rose from the crowd, that same panic that she heard when Lunareth was attacked, the same sharp edge of fear that lingered after losing everything.

The commotion grew louder, the voices grew stronger under the rainfall. But before long, a long line of golden-armored guards filtered into their quarter, quickly dispersing the unrest and detaining those whose voices shouted loudest. They surrounded Jesenia's people, shoulder-to-shoulder, halberds crossed to keep anyone from escaping.

Their superior barked, his voice cold and clipped: "Ingrates! You will not bring your unrest to these streets! You are not citizens, our stores owe you no grain."

Voices began to rise again in protest, and the guards tightened their line. One of them even used the blunt end of his halberd to push one of the elders to the ground. Jesenia was quick to help him back to his feet. The guards' hands tightened around their weapons as the air grew tense with hatred.

And then, everything went quiet. The guards dropped to one knee in unison, and even Jesenia's people seemed to bow. The king moved into the center of the ring without a word, his wings folded close as if to make himself smaller against the world.

When he stopped, the guards rose to their feet, hands still tense on their halberds.

"Lower your weapons," Val-Theris said softly. The order

wasn't barked, it was whispered, and still, the guards obeyed without hesitation.

But their unease was simply masked beneath obedience.

The higher-ranking guard cleared his throat. "Your Majesty, the quarter was out of control. We must secure the square–"

"By shoving down the elderly? By arresting the hungry?"

"With respect, my lord, these are not your people. If we allow them to–"

Val-Theris's voice was quiet but unyielding, each word spoken with deliberate, unshakable certainty. "They are in my city, by my order. That makes them mine."

Silence followed, and Jesenia was not sure who looked more shocked by the king's words: the guards, whose loyalty barely masked their prejudice, or the refugees.

Val-Theris stepped with a purpose toward Jesenia and the elder whom she still helped stand steady. This was the closest she had ever been to him, close enough to pluck a feather from his wings if she dared to.

"Are you alright?" he asked the elder, who simply nodded in response. Val-Theris returned a subtle tilt of the head and then turned away, but not before his piercing gaze found Jesenia's eyes once more.

FIVE

After three weeks, the rations grew thin again. The people of Solmiris grew once again impatient with the Lunarethians, and though her people tried their best to belong, to earn their keep, no one in the city gave them the chance.

Jesenia had finished singing the orphans to sleep, searching for an empty space on the streets to rest herself, when she heard whispers and hushed tones slipping from an alley.

The voices were impossible to discern at first, but as Jesenia crept closer, she overheard the voices of two men.

"It will happen before the next council convenes."

"Who would believe the pacifist filth would make an attempt on the king?"

"The people will believe what they see, and our coffers run deep enough to paint the truth."

She didn't stay to hear more. Jesenia slipped away from the alley, her pulse climbing with each echoing footstep as she ascended the city toward the Golden Citadel.

She could not see their faces, but the way they spoke of her people made it clear that they had to have been Solmiris citizens.

Whatever their grievances were, their intent was unmistakable: they wanted to stage an assassination of the king. And she knew in her bones that if they succeeded, the refugees would be the ones paying the price, no matter their innocence.

Jesenia's legs ached from climbing the steps toward the citadel, but her speed did not falter. She did not know when this council would convene, but she knew it had to be soon, and so she could not hold onto this information for even a moment.

The great citadel rose like golden fire at the top of the hill, vast and gleaming. Its gilded columns caught the soft moonlight so brilliantly it hurt to look at. Banners of crimson, ivory and gold unfurled from towers and above archways, pledging loyalty to the Angel-King inside.

The crimson-cloaked guards at the gates shifted as she came into view, their halberds lowering in perfect unison, points mere inches from her chest.

"Halt, foreigner!"

Jesenia's throat was dry from running, and she lifted her trembling hands to move her hair that had been stuck to her brow from sweat. "Please—please, I have to speak to the King. It's urgent."

The guard on the left tilted his head toward her. "Your business?"

"They mean to kill him!" she blurted. "I–I–I don't know who, but I heard them! An attempt would be made on the King's life before the next council. Please—"

"Your kind is not permitted in the upper terraces," one of the guards said, his weapon still poised toward her.

Jesenia flinched at his harsh tone, but stood her ground, forcing the words through the pounding in her chest. "Please, they will kill him! We have to save him!"

The guards paused for a moment, shared a glance, and then—

They *laughed* at her. They laughed at her for a few long,

humiliating moments, before straightening their spines again, disdain returning to their voices.

"Another fanatic," one said.

The other turned his attention back to Jesenia, taking one measured step forward. His arrogant authority leaked from his armor and stance. "You will return to your quarter. The King is in no danger here. You will not bring your unrest into our gilded halls."

The words hit hard, yet she kept going. "But I heard them plotting–"

"Off the streets, refugee. *Now.*"

Jesenia's nails dug into her palms, the feeling of helplessness and the frustration of being taken for a liar swelling beneath her ribs.

"Please, I swear it on my life–"

"Enough! Go home, girl. I will not say it again!"

For a moment, Jesenia stood there, the sheer weight of this information holding her in place. Jesenia turned to walk away, but paused a half-step forward. Her gaze fell over her shoulder, calculating if she could *just* slip in between the two men...

And before she could think about it, she ran, trying to squeeze through the space between them, shouting to anyone who might be nearby.

"Assassins! Assassins in the city! They're coming for the king!"

Her voice drew the attention of servants and other guards. From behind her, an onlooker threw a piece of fruit at her.

"Lunarethian filth!" a man shouted. "Always stirring trouble!"

The guards quickly caught Jesenia by the arm, twisting it behind her back and forcing her to the ground.

"Stop resisting!"

"I'm trying to save him!" she cried. "Please!"

But they didn't want to hear it. They were more concerned

with keeping her quiet than saving the man leading their country. In their eyes, she was just another vagrant shouting lies to try and earn her people favor.

She struggled against their grip, her hair falling loose across her face. The guards held her down when they shackled her wrists together, and as they drug her away, her cries became background noise in a city too proud of itself to listen.

THE CELL WAS small and damp, carved into the stone beneath the eastern barracks. The air smelled of rust and old rain; each drop from the ceiling struck the floor like a metronome counting down her hours until judgement.

Jesenia sat on the cold stone floor, arms wrapped around her knees. The thin shawl she had brought from Lunareth did little against the chill.

She'd spent the night listening to the muffled echoes of soldiers changing shifts above her, the clatter of armor, the occasional barked order. All of it frightened her, because it meant they were deciding what to do with her.

She was sure she had done the right thing in trying to warn them. Her body moved before her mind could stop her, but she should have known they wouldn't believe her. Not even if she swore it on her life or all the stars in the sky.

They had only listened long enough to have reason to arrest her.

Inciting unrest, they called it. *Disturbing the peace.*

Jesenia scoffed bitterly at that. *What peace?* The city had been cruel to the Lunarethians from the moment they walked through the gates, isolating them like a sickness waiting to spread.

Many hours passed before a noise at the end of the corridor pulled her head up.

A man soon appeared outside of her cell. He wore no helmet, and even in the dim torchlight, she could tell that his armor was more ornate than the guards that arrested her, but nowhere near as intricate as the king's. He must have been a superior. The man's hair was reddish, eyes green, and his clean-shaven face was worn with time, but not unkind. He quietly studied her through the bars for a moment.

"What is your name, Lunarethian?" he asked at last. His voice was deep and even and commanding, but it lacked the cruelty so many of the other guards spoke to her with.

She hesitated. "Jesenia."

He nodded, his expression something like pity. "I am the Angelicus Prime, Rohannes."

Jesenia was quiet with confusion, for she had never heard such a title. He sensed her lack of understanding, quietly adding, "I am the highest ranking officer of the *Angelicus Hastati*. I am here on behalf of His Majesty."

"I only tried to save his life," she said sharply before he could continue. "If that is a crime in this city, then keep me in these chains."

Rohannes tilted his head. "Chains do not make your words false." Before Jesenia could comprehend what he said, he unlocked the door without another word. "Come."

"Why?"

"Because you have been summoned," he said dryly.

Jesenia stood slowly, her legs stiff from the long night. She held out her arms, expecting to be bound again, but he only gestured for her to follow him.

They walked through the narrow hallways in silence. The further they went, the warmer the air became—the scent of burning oil replacing mildew, the faint hum of voices returning. The shift from dungeon to palace felt dizzying.

The throne room doors loomed ahead, sunlight spilling through the cracks like molten gold. Jesenia squinted her eyes at it, her pulse pounding in her ears.

Rohannes rested a hand on the door handle, his voice low. "Mind your tongue, Lunarethian," he warned, before pushing the doors open.

Light flooded around her, and Jesenia stepped forward, semi-blinded by it. She felt small beneath the vaulted, domed ceiling, the air perfumed faintly with incense, the floors polished clean until they held her reflection.

And then she saw him.

The great Angel-King Val-Theris stood near the tall windows overlooking the back side of his citadel, his wings drawn close, each feather pale fire against the dying light. He didn't turn as she approached, but somehow she knew he'd felt her presence.

"Alive," she whispered to herself.

"Your Majesty," Rohannes said from behind her. "I bring you Jesenia of Lunareth, as requested."

Jesenia was unsure whether to bow or speak, so she simply stood in the center of the room. When he finally turned to face her, his expression was unreadable.

"There was an attempt on my life this morning."

Her breath caught in her throat.

"They were stopped," he continued, voice low, steady. His gaze lingered on her face, searching, as though looking for something he could not name. "You tried to warn me."

She swallowed hard, forcing the words past the tightness in her throat. "I—I heard whispers. I thought if I came here…"

"They told me you came to the gates." Something like regret shadowed his features then, faint but unmistakable. "My guards serve me, and so their actions were mine. And I turned you away."

She shook her head quickly. "Your guards did what they thought was right." Her voice was so quiet, carefully minding her words as instructed. At last, Val-Theris stepped closer, his movements smooth and deliberate, until the faint glow of the windows cast him in warm, fractured light. The feathers of his wings shifted gently, catching particles of dust in their wake.

"You could have done nothing," he said. "You could have let whatever was coming find me. Instead, you tried to stop it. For that, I owe you a debt."

Jesenia blinked, startled. "I didn't do it for a reward."

"I know," he said, a faint ghost of softness touching his mouth. Not quite a smile, not quite sorrow. He studied her for a long moment, and then said simply: "One favor, Lady Jesenia. Anything within my power to give is yours."

The words landed like stones in still water, rippling outward. A thousand desperate thoughts surged through her head: jobs for her people, safety for the quarter, passage away from Solmiris entirely. She thought of the murmurs in dark alleys, the angry citizens sharpening knives in silence, the refugees' unrest always one spark away from being set ablaze.

And yet, when she finally found her voice, she heard herself say, softly: "I would ask only for a warm meal for my people."

Val-Theris's brow furrowed faintly, as though he wasn't certain he'd heard her correctly. "A warm meal?" She nodded, forcing herself to meet his gaze. He continued to look at her, stunned. "You could have asked for anything. Wealth. Jewels. Property. Yet you ask for a meal."

Jesenia averted her gaze, humiliation staining her cheeks red. "I meant no offense."

For a moment, he said nothing. The silence stretched, quiet but sharp, and Jesenia felt the weight of his attention in every shallow breath. Then Val-Theris inclined his head once, solemnly, as though she'd asked for something vast and sacred rather than simple and small.

"Done," he said softly.

Her throat ached with words she couldn't find, gratitude burning hot beneath her ribs. She wanted to thank him, but as quickly she had been summoned, Rohannes led her out of the room, and Val-Theris turned his back to her.

Outside, the city's unrest lingered, but in the weight of the king's promise, Jesenia felt the faintest shift in her, that maybe he hadn't abandoned her people entirely.

SIX

VAL-THERIS SAT AT HIS DESK. The ink on the parchment across the table had dried hours ago, unread and forgotten. The reports from the council were stacked high: trade disputes, unrest in the markets, whispers of resentment festering among the people since the refugees' arrival.

And yet, his thoughts returned again and again to the woman from Lunareth—the one who had shouted his name at the gates, the one who had warned him of a blade meant for his throat.

In truth, Val-Theris and his loyal men had already heard the same whispers and were prepared for any strike in his direction.

She could have chosen silence. But instead, she selflessly tried to warn him.

He lifted his head from his fingers slightly when the door opened and the Angelicus Prime stepped in, the sound of his boots muted by the fine rug.

"My king," the captain said, bowing his head.

"Rohannes," Val-Theris began, his voice low, thoughtful. "The foreign girl who was arrested just last night, Jesenia of Lunareth. You recall her?"

"I do."

"I would have you watch her."

Rohannes blinked, not expecting the order. "Watch her, sir?"

Val-Theris's gaze lifted from the papers, the faint light from the brazier catching in his eyes. "Yes. Follow her movements for a few days. Be discreet about it. I would like to know if she is what she appears to be, or if she hides sharper edges beneath all that grace."

Rohannes hesitated. "You believe her to be dangerous?"

"No," Val-Theris said simply. "But selfless people are rarely what they seem. You will return with a full report in three days."

Rohannes bowed his head, retreating from the room in silence, leaving Val-Theris to once again close his eyes and force himself to see Jesenia's face in the marble.

THE LOWER MARKETS of Solmiris had changed since the refugees came. Once a place of uniformity and precision, was now a place of color and noise. The Lunarethians had used old fabric from skirts to decorate their tents in oranges and blues and yellows, for it was all they had to make the stone streets of Solmiris feel like home.

What citizens passed through the refugee quarter stared and mocked, straying far away from any of the Lunarethians. Between them stretched an invisible line of distrust that none of them dared to cross.

The king had asked Rohannes, no, *commanded him*, to keep an eye on the foreign girl. So here he was, three days into his shadowed surveillance, following Jesenia of Lunareth, who seemed determined to make saints look lazy.

At first glance, she was nothing but a worn shawl and shoes held together by twine. But as he watched her, it was the smallest of actions that caught Rohannes off guard. She moved through the crowd like someone who was used to taking up less space, yet always found it in her to help others stand taller.

He watched her kneel beside an old man struggling with a cart of firewood, her hands red from the effort as she helped him stack it. Later, she shared her water with a child who had spilled theirs, then gave away the bread ration she'd just been given to an elderly woman too weak to stand in line. By dusk, she had nothing left but her shawl, which she draped around a coughing boy's shoulders before disappearing into the alleys.

Rohannes followed her there, silent as a shadow.

She knelt beside one of the makeshift fires the Lunarethians kept burning at night, warming her palms from the chill in the air.

The firelight caught her face then. Not beautiful in the way poets described, but luminous in its sincerity. There was a strength there Rohannes recognized, the same kind that kept his soldiers on their feet long after hope had left them.

He stayed until the fire burned low, until most of the camp had drifted to sleep.

Only Jesenia remained awake, sitting near the embers, her hands cupped around the faint warmth as though she could protect it from the night.

Rohannes stood once more before the king's desk, the smell of smoke from the oil lamps curling in the air between them. He looked tired; his cloak was still dusted with dirt from the lower district.

"Well?" Val-Theris asked quietly, setting aside the parchment he hadn't really been reading. "What did you see?"

Rohannes was silent for a moment before answering, as though searching for the right words.

"I watched her for three days as instructed," he said finally. "At dawn she helps the old and sick at the refugee tents. By day she teaches the children of her people anything she knows: their letters, the phases of the moon, songs. She gives away most of what she has, sometimes–*oftentimes*–even her own rations. She just…gives."

He exhaled, shaking his head. "I thought at first it was an act. Some attempt to earn your favor. But she does it even when no one is looking. Never once did she mention your name. She did not curse our city or our people. If anything, she makes us look like savages, the way we've forced them into a cramped corner of our city and forced them to live on less than we give to the criminals awaiting trial."

Val-Theris leaned back in his chair, fingers steepled. "And what is your judgment, Captain?"

"If I didn't know better, I'd say she's trying to atone for the whole world's sins."

Val-Theris was silent for a long moment, staring at the flame between them. "Did she seem to have any family among the refugees?"

"None that I could tell. She walks alone at night," Rohannes continued softly. "Talks to the sick, checks on the children sleeping near the fire pits. When one of them cries, she stays until they stop. It's as though she's trying to hold what's left of her people together with her bare hands." He paused. "It's like she's a blessing from the moon."

Val-Theris's expression didn't change, but something in his shoulders eased. "A patron saint of the pitiful," he whispered to himself. He looked toward the high arched window, where dawn was beginning to brighten the sky. For a long while, neither spoke. At last, Val-Theris said, "Thank you, Rohannes. That will be all."

Rohannes studied him for a long moment before speaking again, his voice edged with curiosity. "You've seen her before, haven't you?"

"Yes," Val-Theris replied softly.

But Rohannes didn't ask when or how, because he saw the look in his king's pale gaze: the devastation of what had not yet come to pass.

SEVEN

IT WAS mid-day when the sound of wheels grinding on stone filled the streets, and carts came into view of the refugee quarter.

Jesenia stood out of the way, in an enclave made by two of the high walls of Solmiris connecting. Her hands were gripping the worn edge of her shawl, watching the procession of golden-armored soldiers push their way through the narrow streets with carts following them.

The scent reached the refugees first. Fresh bread. Roasted meat. Hearty broth. Clean water. The refugees gathered slowly and cautiously, as if unsure if this was a test or some cruel trick. Whispers rippled through the crowd, disbelief so clear in their hopeful voices:

The palace sent this? A blessing from the King! What if it's poisoned? Why would they do this now?

Jesenia felt those questions sharp in her chest. She knew it wasn't unprompted charity, but a debt being paid—a promise being kept. But the bread was fresh, and the meat was hot. It was real enough for her.

When the carts finally opened, the crowd surged forward,

trying their best to keep order despite their bellies crying for relief. Jesenia watched as her people savored every drop of broth and every crumb of bread. For the first time since they arrived, the Lunarethian's looked alive.

But she knew it was temporary.

Her eyes were pulled to a flash of white across the square. Val-Theris stood there, half-hidden in the shadow of his guards, watching her people wait for their rations. No unrest. No climbing over each other to be first in line. No fights over who got a bigger piece of bread.

She watched him for a while, to observe his face. She searched for disgust, or arrogance, or cruelty hidden behind a halo of gold, but she found none. Then, his gaze found hers from across the crowd. He slightly tilted his head to her, to offer wordlessly that he had kept his promise.

She wanted to bow her head back in respect and thanks, but Jesenia knew that by this time tomorrow, her people would be starving again. She could not find it in her heart to be grateful for that.

The guards continued to hand out the bread and soup and meat to the Lunarethians, looking as though the task was beneath them. Their armor caught splashes of sunlight, but there was no warmth in the reflection. They were careful to avoid the gazes of the refugees, and Jesenia could see it plain as day: they did not think her people deserved even a single meal.

Her gaze shifted back to the king, who was speaking with the Angelicus Prime, the man who escorted her from the prison cell. Val-Theris's wings shifted restlessly against his back, as if they were itching to get away from her people, too.

Jesenia hesitated a moment, then approached him, weaving carefully through the crowd until she reached the *Hastati* formation. One of them stepped forward as she did, his halberd angled slightly downward in warning.

"Let her through," Val-Theris said from behind them, his voice soft. The guard stepped back immediately and shifted his body to allow her to pass through the line. Jesenia quietly stepped forward, her hands tightening around her shawl again.

Now that she was closer, she could see that the king looked even more tired than before, shadows pooling beneath his eyes where his radiance did not linger. He was still turned slightly away from her, but she somehow knew he was listening.

"I just wanted to say…" she paused, swallowing back the sudden emotion in her throat. "Thank you."

His gaze shifted to her then. "I made you a promise," he said simply. She wanted to say more, but his words didn't seem to invite any more conversation. "This will not make things easier," he added. "There are many who see this as an indulgence, and others…" his gaze flickered to the refugees, "that would say it is not enough."

"I know," Jesenia replied. "But I shall remember who gave it to them."

For a moment, he only studied her, the light of the high sun catching on the planes of his face, and filtering through the feathers of his wings. Val-Theris's expression softened, faintly, and he gestured with his hand for her to step away with him. "Do you have a moment?"

Jesenia said nothing, but followed him a few paces away from the guards and the Angelicus Prime—but she could still feel their heavy gazes on her back.

"My people grow restless with the Lunarethian presence here within my walls," he said. When he saw Jesenia's head lower, he added: "I don't tell you this to make you feel shame, but because it is the truth. I can command soldiers, but grain, property, water—those things are governed by my council, and I cannot begin to mend what I do not understand. You live among your people, and you hear what I do not. Tell me, Lady Jesenia, what is it your people need from Solmiris?"

Her fingers began to fiddle with the fabric of her skirt. There was so much to say to the king who sought to understand her people, and yet, when she met his gaze, the words that escaped her lips were an answer neither of them expected.

"They want to go home."

Val-Theris furrowed his brow. "Home."

She drew in a breath. "You've given us your grace by letting us in the walls, given us safety when we had nowhere else to go. But Solmiris isn't ours, and it will never be. My people want your war to end so we can return to Lunareth. To our markets. To the stone houses built by their forefathers and the graves of their mothers. We don't want to stay here fighting for scraps of food any more than your people want to spare the grain."

He stood up straighter, his wings shifting faintly. "I'm sorry I did not see before that Korvath didn't just burn Lunareth, but took your hearts with them, too."

Jesenia saw grief beneath all the command and certainty he radiated. "We do not fault you for that, we know who took our homes from us. But every morning we wake up under your banners, and we're reminded of what's been lost." She swallowed. "Have you ever been to Lunareth, sir?"

"No," he admitted shamefully.

Jesenia gave him a soft, but sorrowful smile as her eyes misted over. "We had celebrated the Festival of First Light just hours before the attack. Nearly three-thousand of us crowded into the streets. Dancing, drinking, laughing. We lost twenty-two people on the road here. Do you know how many of us are left?"

Val-Theris shook his head.

"Ninety-three arrived here at your gates. I counted this morning; eighty-nine remain."

He was quiet then, studying her with a focus so intense it felt like standing directly beneath a beam of light. At last, he said softly: "I am sorry, Lady Jesenia, that Solmiris has failed your people. I asked to speak with you because I had hoped you would speak freely with me about your people, but I have found now that you speak with more clarity than my entire council. You have reminded me of what I serve, and that is all who live within my city, however temporary."

While his words sat heavy on her heart, Jesenia took notice that he did not promise change. Something unspoken lingered between them, and when neither of them spoke again, she bowed her head and turned away.

Before she stepped through the line of guards, she turned back to find Val-Theris had rejoined the Angelicus Prime, and both of their gazes watched her with a depth she had no words to explain.

When Jesenia returned to the square, the food was nearly gone, laughter rising from voices that had forgotten it for too long. Children clutched pieces of bread in both hands, the old sat cross-legged on the stones, murmuring blessings Jesenia hadn't heard since Lunareth fell.

But when she glanced back to the edge of the square, Val-Theris was already leaving, his guards falling into step around him, crimson capes dissolving into the gilded glow of the upper district, ready to forget about her and her people once more.

EIGHT

THE RAIN HAD TURNED the lower courtyard into a pit of mud and puddles. Refugees lined up by the dozens, shivering beneath thin cloaks, their breath misting in the cold from the turn of the seasons. The smell of wet cloth and the constant low rumble of hungry bellies clung to the air.

At the front of the line, the *Hastati* distributed rations—half-filled ladles of thin, cold soup and stale bread. One by one, as orderly as could be, the Lunarethians shuffled forward for their share. Though the guards upturned their noses at their dirty clothes and accented vowels, the Lunarethians still murmured soft thanks.

Jesenia was last in the line, ensuring all the children and elderly had managed to get their rations first. By the time Jesenia reached the front, the guards had grown tired and irritable. The ladle scraped against the large pot, nearly empty. She waited patiently for them to scrape out whatever broth was left, and held out her bowl for her share. She was soaked to the bone and her hair clung to her cheeks, her hands trembling from the cold.

The guard in charge of the bread—a broad man with a scar

running through his brow—looked at her with open, obvious disdain. "Hmph," he scoffed. "If it isn't His Majesty's savior." He gave her a nasty look. "I think you're due a feast."

Jesenia, foolishly not knowing any better, softened her gaze on him as if she expected him to be kind. When he lifted the ladle to tip it into her bowl, he poured it just short of the dish, spilling the broth all over her bare feet.

Jesenia and the Lunarethians stared at the ground, but no one spoke.

"Clumsy me!" the guard said, his tone mocking sympathy. Then, he reached into the bread basket. He tore a large bite from it for himself, chewing slowly. He swallowed, then smiled. "Had to make sure it wasn't poisoned, right?"

Then, he tossed the mangled hunk of bread into a puddle at her feet.

For a moment, Jesenia just looked at it, then, without a word, she knelt. Her hands shook as she lifted the bread from the ground, wiping away what dirt and water she could before tucking it under her arm. No tears. No anger. She would not give their cruelty the satisfaction of seeing her cry.

The guards laughed and turned away, packing away the ration cart and wheeling it away, boasting about their own hot meals waiting for them at the barracks as if nothing had happened.

But from the shadows, where no one could see, the Angelicus Prime watched.

He had come on the king's orders, to continue his surveillance of Lady Jesenia of Lunareth, but as he watched her take a seat under the bulwark to shield her from the rain and eat her dirty bread with tears streaking down her cheeks, Rohannes felt his stomach twist.

He had fought wars, seen men gutted and burned, but somehow that small, deliberate cruelty from the men he commanded unsettled him more than anything he had seen before. Rohannes turned away from the scene with his jaw clenched. On his way back to the palace, he made a side stop at a bakery.

When Jesenia returned to her makeshift tent of linens crudely strung together that night, she found a full loaf of fresh bread atop a note:

Returned by order of decency.

It was unsigned.

WHEN ROHANNES RETURNED to the throne room, there were only a few braziers still lit. Their flames were low and did little to warm the ache in his heart for what he had witnessed in the refugee quarter.

Val-Theris was pacing at the foot of the dais, his wings twitching—a sign that he was deep in thought. He did not look up as Rohannes approached.

"I sense your tension. What troubles you?" the king asked quietly.

Rohannes hesitated, rain still dripping from his cloak. "Forgive me sir, but I fear you would not believe me if I told you."

That gave Val-Theris pause. "Tell me anyway," he said, still pacing.

So Rohannes did; he spoke plainly of what he saw, trying his best to leave the emotions he was feeling out of it, for it was not his job to feel. He told his king about the cruelty of the guards and how Lady Jesenia hadn't let them break her there, only to cry into her bread when they left.

When he finished his report, the silence between them was nearly suffocating. Val-Theris clasped his hands behind his back and stood straighter, his chin tilted upward with authority. "And no one stopped it?"

"No, sir."

"Not even you?"

"No, sir."

For a moment, it was quiet, but Val-Theris finally spoke, his piercing eyes burning with a quiet fury—at his men, at Rohannes, at himself.

"Tell them they are summoned. Now."

It did not take long for Rohannes to find them. They were where they said they'd be: enjoying a warm meal and cold mead in the barracks. They were brought before the king, Rohannes behind them to face the same shame.

Val-Theris entered the throne room slowly, his boots reverberating against the polished marble, his wings spread wide as a silent intimidation. They seemed to fill the room with light, but it was not radiant or divine—it was cold and pale.

"My soldiers are the heart of Seraveth, the hand of the great city of Solmiris. When I cannot be everywhere, you are to serve as my eyes, my conscience, and above all, my honor." Val-Theris came to a stop in front of the three. His eyes paused on Rohannes, the disappointment evident in them. "Tell me—when you spilled soup on a hungry woman's feet, was it my hand you acted with? When you laughed at her, was it my voice you echoed?"

The older of the two guards swallowed hard. "Your Majesty, it was a lapse in judgement."

Val-Theris's expression didn't soften. "That was no apology, but then again, it is not I that deserves it." He turned to

Rohannes, who stood behind them, frozen heavy with shame. "These men acted beneath my banner, but it was your eyes that observed the act. Their punishment should be yours to decide. As for you, I expected better from the Angelicus Prime. My disappointment is immeasurable."

Rohannes nodded, observing the arrogance of his men, the faint disbelief that they were being judged at all. Then, he took a deep breath.

"Your Majesty, I propose myself and these men be stripped of our sigils for one week's time, and should spend that time in the refugee quarter as their equals to learn what we have broken."

Val-Theris said nothing as Rohannes proposed his judgement, he simply nodded in agreement. "I trust you can make the arrangements yourself," he said to the Angelicus Prime.

He bowed his head, and instructed the guards to follow him to the barracks where they would turn in their armor, weapons, and sigils of authority.

When the doors closed behind them, the silence was thick in the air. Val-Theris sunk into the steps, wings drooping, the tension in his shoulders revealing his exhaustion.

THE NEXT MORNING was gray and heavy with mist. The fires warming and lighting the Lunarethian quarter smoldered low, and the air smelled of ash, damp linen, and wet stone.

Rohannes and his men, dressed in simple trousers and pants, walked into the quarter quietly. Their clean, high-quality clothes stood out amongst the rags the refugees wore, for their clothing had worn through during their travels to Solmiris, and they had no funds to replace them.

Rohannes led them through the quarter until they found who they were looking for, huddled under a tarp, mending a hole in a quilt with another refugee. Jesenia saw them approach from the corner of her eye, recognizing that they were not Lunarethian, but not immediately realizing it was Rohannes or the men who had acted cruelly the day before.

"Lady Jesenia," he said respectfully.

She stood and came closer, finally recognizing them. She folded her shawl around her shoulders uncomfortably. "Yes?"

Rohannes gestured to his men, who scowled, but approached. One of them spoke. "We have come to apologize for our actions yesterday."

"We have disgraced our city and our king," the other added.

Rohannes then cleared his throat. "We have come to assist your people for the next week. We have been stripped of our titles and authority until this week's end, so while we cannot provide more food or supplies, we can help your sick, watch the children, tend the fires. Whatever you need from us, we shall see that it is done."

There was no triumph nor bitterness in Jesenia's eyes. There was simply the calm composure of a woman who had long ago decided that hate was too toxic a poison to carry in her heart. She blinked up at Rohannes. "Are you here to watch over them?"

"No, my lady. I am here as part of my punishment as well."

"*Your* punishment?" she asked.

"For watching them, and doing nothing to stop it."

Jesenia paused for a moment—realization striking her as she understood he must have been the one to leave her the bread. "I see."

She inclined her head for the men to follow. She led them deeper into the camp. She did not berate them or remind them of their cruelty, she simply approached a thin, feverish child resting on his mother's lap. She took the child into her own lap and rocked him as the mother's eyes shut for rest, knowing her son was safe.

Jesenia's eyes turned to the guards and Rohannes, then pointed toward an elderly man coughing into a rag. "Work," she instructed.

Rohannes was frozen for a moment, exhaling slowly. He watched Jesenia offer the men who had humiliated her a soft smile of encouragement as they tried to keep themselves busy. No scorn. Just…patience and goodwill.

"*Pacifists*," he muttered to himself. "Val-Or help me, maybe they've been right all along…"

A younger Lunarethian child approached Rohannes then, holding out a small piece of torn parchment shyly. He hesitated, but crouched so their eyes met as he took the paper.

Thank you.

Rohannes looked up and caught Jesenia's gaze. She didn't smile, but nodded once at him in acknowledgement.

NINE

Night had fallen heavy over Solmiris. The palace glowed like a dying ember in the distance. Its marble halls were half-lit, its golden windows reflecting a light that no longer felt divine.

Val-Theris sat alone in his council chamber, sleeves rolled up, fingers tracing the edge of an untouched parchment. He had dismissed the court hours ago but hadn't moved since.

When the doors opened after a brief knock, he didn't look up.

"Report," he said simply.

Rohannes entered, his boots clicking softly against the marble. His armor was unpolished, his face still dusted with the grit of the refugee quarter he had spent the last week in. He stopped a few paces away. "The sentence was carried out as ordered."

"And?"

Rohannes hesitated, unsure where to begin. Finally, he said, "We worked the entire week. Fed the sick. Buried the dead. Slept among the refugees. Lady Jesenia led us herself."

Her name drew Val-Theris's gaze. "She led you?"

"Aye," Rohannes said. "From the moment we arrived until the last day ended."

Val-Theris leaned back slowly in his chair, the faintest flicker of something in his eyes—surprise, perhaps, or even disbelief. "And she didn't…retaliate?"

Rohannes shook his head. "Not once. No anger, no pride. She spoke to us like equals. Like…students, almost." He paused, thinking. "She showed us what compassion looks like better than anyone I've ever met, Majesty."

The king rose from his chair and crossed the room, his shadow stretching long across the stone floor. He stopped by the window, looking out over the distant glow of the lower city. Faint, golden, flickering with the small fires of the refugee camps.

"She's teaching my men mercy," he murmured. "While I sit here debating how to enforce it."

Rohannes tilted his head slightly. Val-Theris turned, the light from the braziers catching on the gold of his hair, the exhaustion in his eyes more profound than usual.

"She has no title," he said quietly. "No wealth, no station, no voice within these walls. And yet, when she speaks, people listen. They obey."

He stepped away from the window, pacing slowly, his thoughts spilling into words almost without meaning to. "I thought mercy was something to be enforced. A law of the crown. But she—" He exhaled. "She carries it as if it's her duty."

Rohannes allowed himself a faint smile. "You sound jealous."

Val-Theris's lips curved faintly. "Perhaps I am." He turned back to the desk and rested both hands upon it, the flickering light from the candles gilding the edges of his wings. "Tomorrow," he said finally. "I will summon the council for a special session."

Rohannes frowned. "Majesty?"

"I will offer Jesenia of Lunareth a seat among them to speak for her people."

Rohannes's brows lifted slightly. "They'll protest." Val-Theris hummed in acknowledgement and sank back into his chair. "Do you think she'll accept?" Rohannes asked.

Val-Theris did not look up. "Not at first. She'll tell me she's not made for courts or councils. That she's no one important." He paused, gaze distant. "But she'll come," he said softly. "Because she can't stand to see suffering and stay silent when she has the chance to change it."

THE COUNCIL CHAMBER smelled faintly of beeswax and light smoke from the cigars hanging from the mouths of Seraveth's most influential men. The marble floors reflected soft ribbons of light, but the air was heavy—always weighed down by the never-ending divisiveness of old arguments.

Val-Theris stood at the far end of the table, pale wings folded tight against his back as the council spoke over one another in restless waves of frustration.

As king, Val-Theris had the right to open the meeting with whichever issue he chose, though he rarely exercised that right. But with the Lunarethian's within their walls, he felt it pressing to do something to ease their suffering. He could not propose rations or shelter—his councilmen would never allow it, but he had come up with a plan that involved neither.

"I will be taking the Angelicus Prime to Korvath to negotiate a ceasefire with Val-Oros," Val-Theris said to the chamber, which had grown silent when he began to speak. "It is my intention to ask him to remove his men from the Lunarethian region so that its people may return home."

There was little pushback from the councilors at this proposal, and the matter was settled. But Val-Theris knew his next proposal would alight infighting the chamber had not seen in decades.

"Secondly," he began, "Until a time comes when the refugees can return to their homes, they should have a seat at this table. I have decided I will offer the position to Jesenia of Lunareth, who has shown a great deal of loyalty and respect to the people of Solmiris, and to me."

The chamber was silent for a moment, and then it erupted with protest.

"Your Grace, with respect, this matter requires delicacy."

"Delicacy does not mean handing influence to an outsider—"

"Especially not one from *their* quarter."

Val-Theris's gaze remained steady on the carved marble surface of the table, letting them speak, letting the tide of their voices crash into him. At last, he lifted his head.

Councilor Varin, one of the eldest among them, leaned forward with his hands clasped and his knuckles pressing into wood. "My lord," he said carefully, "we are sworn to serve you. To advise you. To act as the spine of this city when darkness grows long. And yet—" He hesitated, measuring his words. "And yet, when unrest grows in the quarter, you summon one of those unruly vagrants. And a woman, no less!"

The chamber filled with murmurs of agreement.

The memory of Jesenia's voice still lingered in Val-Theris's mind, soft but unyielding as she'd said: *They just want to go home.*

He felt the ripple of quiet judgment settle around the table and folded his wings tighter, his hands curling loosely at his sides.

"She has the trust of her people," Val-Theris said, his tone even, controlled. "She hears what none of you will hear and sees what none of you choose to see. Her counsel is—"

"Dangerous," Varin interrupted, sharper now, his restraint faltering. "You raise her voice above ours, and they will raise her name above yours. She is not one of us, Val-Theris. She does not serve Seraveth. She serves *them*. Do not confuse her decency with loyalty."

A younger but still seasoned councilor spoke then, low and measured, each word chosen like a blade: "The people already murmur, my lord. They see where your gaze lingers. They see who commands your loyal men through punishment inside the gates. Give our people no reason to believe your judgment... compromised."

Silence fell. Val-Theris's jaw tightened, shadows curling low beneath his lashes as he let the words settle, cold and sharp in the room's stillness. The weight of command sat heavily against his shoulders, and though his wings remained steady, he felt the faint tremor in his hands.

He dismissed the council then, voice soft and expression unreadable, but their words clung long after their footsteps faded into the vaulted corridors.

Moments later, Rohannes approached his king, having witnessed the session from the corner.

"So we are to leave for Korvath, sir?" he asked quietly, careful not to mention Jesenia or Lunareth.

Val-Theris nodded. "Gather a few of your best men to accompany us. You will leave tonight—bring my horse with you. I am going to fly to Lunareth and see what my brother has done with my own eyes. I will meet you there tomorrow morn."

Rohannes bowed at the instructions and left to make the arrangements. While his wings allowed him to travel the journey in less than two days, Val-Theris did not want to meet his brother alone. Val-Oros and Val-Theris were blessed with immortal life from their father, but could still be killed, and the only men foolish enough to try to end their lives were each other.

Val-Theris finally left the chamber and retreated to his private quarters in the eastern wing of the palace. He stood out over his city on the same balcony where he had countless visions, hoping, this time, for another of Jesenia.

The thought startled him, like he hadn't meant to think it in the first place. He knew nothing of her other than the honesty and kindness she had shown him and his men, and yet the Angel-King stood there, yearning to see her gentle face in his mind.

Val-Theris stood at the edge of what had once been a city, his wings folded neat against his back, their gold dulled beneath the gray sky. The air smelled of ash and old rain, of stone burned too long and never rebuilt. No birds cried here. No insects stirred. Even the light seemed reluctant to linger.

Houses lay collapsed into themselves, roof beams charred black, doorways yawning open as if still waiting for their owners to return. The streets were carved with scars from flame, deep grooves etched where boots and chains had passed in endless procession.

He saw scorch marks at child's height along the walls and turned away.

He knelt beside a shattered well, its stones cracked and split, and pressed his palm to the earth. The ground was cold. Empty. It gave nothing back.

My war did this to them, he thought. A war he never wanted, but also a war he never seemed to fight hard enough to win.

Further in, the central square opened before him, wide and ruined. Scattered around lay remnants of life hastily left behind: a child's shoe half-buried in soot, a cooking pot warped by heat, a length of fabric snagged on a nail, fluttering weakly in the wind.

And bones. So many bones.

Val-Theris's chest ached.

At the far end of the square, tangled in the debris of a collapsed wall, he saw a banner. It was torn, its edges scorched, the silver sigil of Lunareth barely visible beneath ash and grime.

He approached slowly as though nearing the body of a fallen soldier.

With careful hands, he freed the banner from the rubble. He shook it once, gently, letting the dust fall away, then folded it, taking care to preserve what little remained unmarred. His movements were almost ritualistic, as though this small act might atone for the thousands he could never save.

"I see you," he murmured, though no one remained to hear it. "I will remember you."

He tucked the folded banner beneath his arm and rose, turning one last time to survey the ruin.

This was not a battlefield. This was a wound carved into the earth and soaked with the blood of people who never would have fought back.

As he lifted into the air, wings beating softly against the cold sky, Val-Theris understood something with terrible clarity: no ceasefire, no treaty, no victory would ever undo what had been taken from Lunareth.

It was a burden of truth that rested solely on his shoulders—a failure branded into the very earth.

THE DESERT WIND howled as Val-Theris's convoy crossed the blackened threshold into Korvath. The sky here was the color of ash, the sun dimmed by a haze that seemed to rise from the ground itself.

Korvath's capital—*the Citadel of Thorns*—sprawled before them. Its iron and stone towers clawed upward, jagged and sharp, catching the light as though built to wound the heavens themselves.

A Korvathian scout had seen them on the horizon, and so it was no shock when Val-Theris's brother greeted them at the unholy gates.

"Welcome home, brother," Val-Oros said, his voice echoing with pride and something darker. His wings burned red in the half-light, the tips blackened like cooled embers.

Home. His words were not untrue, but they still struck Val-Theris like a blade to the heart. They had lived and ruled this land together once, before their opposing morality drove them apart. Korvath looked much different than when he had last seen it—his gaze drifted to the streets behind them, lined with people that were thin, gray, and silent.

Children carried buckets of water heavier than their arms could bear. Men were in chains, scrubbing dirt from the ground and buildings. Women knelt beside the roads as if in silent prayer, faces veiled, bowing to Val-Oros as he led the Seravethians inward to his palace.

"Why are they all so quiet?" Val-Theris asked his brother, gesturing to the women who bowed.

Val-Oros gave him a wicked smile and threw his arm over his shoulder. "Because they have no tongues."

Val-Theris halted. "That is a cruel jest."

His brother's grin widened. "I have no reason to jest. Our women are silenced as soon as they have their first bleed. It keeps order. Women are the first to gossip, the first to protest, the first to whine. I wish to hear none of it."

He said it so casually that Val-Theris felt his spine go numb. His wings flared unconsciously, a ripple of gold and white amongst the gray and suffering. "You mutilate them?"

Val-Oros shrugged. "I *perfect* them."

He led Val-Theris and his convoy through the city. For the Angel-King, it was like a descent into Hell. For Val-Oros, he described it all as if it was something to be proud of.

Workers in the fields harvested fruit and vegetables under lash and flame. Young boys were being trained to fight with barbed chains around their throats. Women with babies were huddled into a tiny shack in the furthest corner of the city so that no one heard the crying. The rest of them were treated like cattle—but Val-Theris thought to himself that even Korvath's livestock were granted more dignity than their women. There was an entire district of men that were maimed and blind. Val-Oros called them *the Unworthy*, stripped of name and purpose, left alive only as a warning to others not to disappoint their king.

When they finally reached the palace after their tour, Val-Theris was offered a meal, but he felt too sick to eat. The banquet table was filled to the brim with feast, but all he could smell was blood, fire, and dirt. Even his men barely picked at their plates. Val-Theris wondered if they considered what a privilege it was to live as freely as they do in Seraveth. Val-Theris was not a perfect ruler, but he certainly wasn't intentionally cruel like his brother.

Val-Oros watched him carefully. In his lap sat two of his

wives, topless, and Val-Theris made a very obvious effort to divert his eyes. They may be called wives, but Val-Theris saw what they really were: slaves.

"Hmph," Val-Oros muttered as he groped the women on his lap. "You judge me, little brother."

"I need to speak with you," he responded.

"So speak," Val-Oros said. He bounced his legs where his wives sat. "Don't worry, they're silent, remember? They won't betray your confidence."

"You need to end your occupation of Lunareth." Val-Theris finally met his brother's eyes. "Its people have done nothing to earn your wrath in this war. Only a weak man targets weak people."

Val-Oros threw his head back and laughed. "Tired of them already? I knew you would be."

"No," Val-Theris said. "They *want* to go home."

"And what if I *want* Lunareth?"

"This is bigger than *our* wants, Val-Oros. People have a right to live and die where they choose to. Have you truly turned so far from our father's Light?"

"Our father expected me to rule, and I have. That is what the Light demanded of me when I was created."

Val-Theris met his gaze, unflinching. "If this is what the Light now demands, then it has gone blind."

"Perhaps that is why you and I were given foresight, brother. To fill in the blind spots where His Light cannot reach."

"I don't think our father intended for us to wage a war against each other," Val-Theris said quietly.

But his brother was no longer listening, busying himself with his wives, and Val-Theris had not the heart to push knowing how far Korvath had fallen under his brother's rule.

That night, he stood on the balcony of his guest chamber.

The capital burned below him with the white-hot sear of humiliation and cruelty.

Rohannes approached quietly, stopping a few paces behind him. "Majesty," he said. "You've seen enough?"

Val-Theris didn't turn. "More than enough."

Rohannes exhaled, his jaw tight. "Korvath isn't a kingdom. It's a tomb."

Val-Theris nodded slowly. "You're right. Korvath must be freed. But I don't know how to help them."

He said it not as a ruler, but as a man who every day grieved the loss of what his brother could have been.

Rohannes hesitated. "And Val-Oros?"

Val-Theris closed his eyes. The vision came like lightning. He saw Val-Oros beaten and bloody. He saw his own hand wrapped around the sword buried in his brother's chest. He staggered back, gasping, his hand clutching the balcony rail as Rohannes held him steady. The vision lingered for a moment too long, the taste of bloody iron on his tongue, the sound of his brother's laugh ending with a crude, harsh breath of pain.

Rohannes reached for him, alarmed. "My king–"

Val-Theris straightened, forcing air into his lungs, forcing calm into his body. But his eyes were distant, already haunted by what was to come.

"I came here to see how he rules," Val-Theris said after a long silence. "And I have." He looked toward Solmiris. "The brother I once stood beside no longer exists," he whispered, the ache in his throat too agonizing to say more.

WHEN VAL-THERIS RETURNED TO SOLMIRIS, his bones were filled with unease and uncertainty. There was much to do: sessions to attend, guard to command, strategies to form. But he had one singular need, and he knew he would be unable to complete any task before this one.

Still in his gear from traveling, he handed off his horse to Rohannes and stepped into the refugee quarter. The Lunarethians parted for him, lowering their eyes and stepping out of his path.

His eyes scanned the small crowds of people for her, and she was where it would have been most obvious to look for her: among the sick. Jesenia held a wet rag to an elderly woman's forehead with a small child on her hip that had a cough.

Val-Theris waited patiently for her to stand, and when she did, her eyes found his instantly. She shifted the child to the opposite hip and quietly approached him.

"Your Majesty," she greeted with a small curtsey, her voice careful. For a moment, her voice eased his shame and the ache in his chest, but it returned like a predictable, steady tide.

Her linen dress was filthy at the bottom, but she stood next to him like she belonged there, as if whatever she said, she knew he would listen.

"You look tired," she said gently. "The people say you traveled to Korvath."

"I did," Val-Theris confirmed. "And that is why I have come. But first–"

He held out a folded piece of cloth to her, in a familiar deep blue. Jesenia handed the child to another woman and then took the cloth from him with a tremble in her hands. She unfolded it as if it were the most precious thing in the world.

When it was fully opened, Jesenia's eyes filled with tears. It was a banner of Lunareth. It was scorched and dirty, but it did not matter, for Jesenia's heart cracked with joy at the sight of something from her home.

"I visited Lunareth on the way to Korvath. I saw what my brother had done to your home, and I'm sorry it took seeing it with my own eyes to understand that devastation. There was… not much left, but I could not leave this behind. I hope you and your people find comfort in this relic and know that Lunareth is not lost."

Jesenia's face was wet when she met his eyes. "This means more to me than I can properly express."

Val-Theris slightly shook his head. "It's alright, I can see it in your eyes. I hope…I'd like to speak with you if you have a moment."

"We are speaking, aren't we?" she asked as she wiped her eyes with her sleeve.

"Yes, but what I have to say cannot fall into the wrong ears."

She blinked at him, then nodded. She carefully, reverently folded the banner and handed it off to be cleaned. Then, she allowed the Angel-King to silently lead her through the city to his palace, where he invited her into his office. Rohannes was already there, waiting.

Val-Theris motioned for her to sit in the chair opposite his desk. He fell into his own chair as if it was the first time he rested his legs in days, and even his wings seemed to limp with exhaustion.

Jesenia began the conversation by asking: "Korvath is worse than the stories, isn't it? I can see it in your eyes."

He tightened his jaw, unsurprised by her ability to understand him with just a look. "It is." She waited for him, giving him space to find the right words. Val-Theris found himself restless once more and rose from his seat, moving toward the balcony where the mid-day breeze spilled through the open doors. His wings caught the sunlight, but their golden sheen seemed dull. "I thought I knew what cruelty was," he began. "But I didn't. I don't. What my brother has built—Korvath is not a kingdom, Lady Jesenia. It is a graveyard that buries the living."

He stared out at his capital city below. "The men labor until their bones break. The children are trained to fight to the death. The women…he mutilates them. And this is only what I saw. I tremble at the thought of what lingered where I couldn't see."

Jesenia pressed a hand to her mouth, feeling sick as horror softened her expression.

"He said it's what the Light demands. That because he was created for rule, that it is the right way to lead. He believes cruelty is the only language worth understanding, the only language that keeps order and peace." He turned to her then, his eyes haunted. "Tell me, Lady Jesenia, how do I save people that can't even ask for help?"

Jesenia thought about it for a long while, the air growing stale between them. "Your brother took their voices," she said. "So you must start by giving them one." He frowned slightly at her answer, but she continued on. "You can't save people by pitying them, Val-Theris. You have to listen—but not just to the loudest. Not to the most powerful. But the ones no one wants to hear. People cannot be saved if they believe there is no hope."

He let out a shaky breath. "You make it sound so simple."

She smiled faintly at him. "Nothing about kindness is simple —not in your position. I understand the burden you bear in wanting to be a compassionate ruler, but Korvath's people will not turn to you if they believe you and your brother are the same man drenched in different light. Isn't that why you built Seraveth? Because your people chose you, and Korvath's people chose your brother."

He looked at her for a long moment, his heart pounding in his chest. "Would you help me, Jesenia? Not just for Korvath, but for Lunareth too. To advise me as someone who knows what it means to have nothing."

Jesenia hesitated. "You want me to counsel you?"

"Yes."

Her throat tightened. "And what if what you believe disagrees with my council?"

He smiled, weary but genuine. "Then fight with me. Argue with me until our throats are sore, but do it for the better of all of our kingdoms."

She stood and moved to stand at his side on the balcony, watching over his city with him. She considered for a long while what it meant to advise a king, and how desperate he must have been to ask in the first place. She was a woman who held no station, power, or wealth, and yet still, he trusted her to be a voice for not just Lunareth, but his brother's country too—at least temporarily.

She tightened her shawl around her shoulders in the breeze. "What if I am not good at it?" she asked quietly, like she was already expecting the criticism to come.

"You've seen more of humanity than all my councilors combined, Lady Jesenia. That makes you more qualified than any of them. And I do not expect you to be perfect—I just hope you can provide perspective to myself and a group of men who have never known anything other than golden spoons. No prophet I've ever known fights for others the way you do."

She tilted her head. "Prophets look to the heavens for answers," she said quietly. "But I found mine in the dirt under my nails."

From behind them, Val-Theris heard Rohannes stifle a laugh, and it brought a faint smile to his own face. In that moment, standing side-by-side above the Golden City, they ceased to be king and foreigner, but man and woman burdened with faith that they could remake the world for the better.

TEN

The council chamber smelled faintly of oil and old ink. It was not an unpleasant scent. It was clean, carefully maintained, but it carried no warmth.

Jesenia noticed it the moment she stepped inside, the way the air seemed to press back against her lungs as if testing whether she belonged there. The chamber was full, every seat occupied, every surface polished to a soft gleam. Sunlight filtered through the tall windows in fractured bands, catching on carved sigils and the gold-thread embroidery of the ministers' robes.

None of it reached the floor where she stood.

Val-Theris moved ahead of her with measured steps, his presence drawing the room's attention as surely as gravity. His wings were folded close, pale feathers layered neatly against his back, their faint glow subdued beneath the weight of the chamber.

Jesenia had dressed carefully. Not *finely*—she had never owned anything that could rival the silks and jewels gathered here. The pastel blue gown she wore was clean and unadorned, its lines simple, its sleeves modest. No ornaments. No attempt to soften herself into something palatable. Her hair was braided back at the nape of her neck, practical and restrained. If they would not see her as an equal, she would at least not give them a spectacle of useless attempts at becoming it.

The murmuring in the chamber slowed as Val-Theris reached the head of the long marble table. He paused there, one hand resting lightly against the stone, and for a moment Jesenia had the strange, unbidden thought that he looked tired. Not in the way soldiers grew weary, but hollowed, as though parts of him had been taken from him slowly, day by day, and never replaced, like the father before him that grew weak with time.

"This is Jesenia of Lunareth," he said. His voice carried easily, steady and low, settling into the chamber without effort. "She will speak for the refugee quarter."

The silence that followed was brief. Then it splintered.

Jesenia felt the subtle shift in posture, the tightening of shoulders, the small, shared glances traded like currency. A cough was stifled. A chair creaked as someone leaned back, too relaxed for the gravity of the moment.

Councilor Myrran's voice cut through first, smooth as oiled steel. "A bold appointment, your Majesty." He reclined in his chair, fingers steepled loosely before him, eyes flicking over Jesenia with open appraisal. "Shall we extend the courtesy further? Invite the farmers next? Or perhaps the beggars? The thieves?"

A ripple of amusement passed the table, restrained but unmistakable. Another voice followed, sharper, younger. *"I was unaware pacifism now qualified as statecraft."*

The laughter that followed was stifled. These men knew better than to be loud, and understood that cruelty carried more weight when delivered politely.

Jesenia did not move in her seat at the king's side. Her hands were folded loosely in her lap, fingers laced together just enough to still their tremor. Val-Theris's jaw tightened.

She felt it beside her, the faint shift of tension radiating from him like heat. His wings twitched once, feathers rustling softly, catching the light in a way that made several councilors glance up despite themselves.

He said nothing to them. The meeting moved on.

When the first matter was raised—grain allocation to the outer wards—Jesenia drew a careful breath and spoke.

The sound of her voice felt too loud in her own ears, though she kept it steady. "The Lunarethian quarter has been surviving on half-rations for months. If supplies from the upper districts were redistributed more evenly, starvation could be prevented before winter turns harsh."

She did not plead. She did not raise her voice. She spoke as one might speak of weather, or of numbers on a ledger, because hunger did not care whether it was acknowledged with passion or not, and neither did these men.

Lord Myrran chuckled softly. "And have Solmiris dine like peasants so peasants may live like kings?"

A councilor with heavy rings sniffed. "Our people earned their prosperity. The refugees have given this city nothing but burden."

Jesenia felt the words land like blows. Dull at first, then sharp as they settled. She swallowed, her throat tightening. "My people gave their homes for your war," she said. "Their families. Their faith. What more would you take from us?"

"Their *silence*," a younger councilor muttered, not quite under his breath.

Someone else laughed. Another voice added, lazily, "Feed them rats. Solve two problems at once."

The sound that followed was not laughter so much as approval of the proposal. For a moment, Jesenia's composure faltered. She felt it physically. A subtle churning of her stomach, a burning warmth behind her eyes she forced back down. She kept her head lifted, her posture straight, even as something inside her curled inward in an attempt to hide.

Beside her, Val-Theris's wings shifted again.

The light around him brightened, just slightly, enough that the nearest councilors fell quiet. Jesenia felt the change like pressure in the air. She knew that he could silence them. That a single word from him would shatter the smug ease in their voices, would remind them exactly who sat at the head of the table.

She waited. So did the council. Val-Theris saw the careful attention too, the subtle nods exchanged between men who had already decided how this would be spun. If he defended her now, they would not hear justice. They would hear favoritism. They would hear confirmation of their quiet rumors: that their king had grown indulgent, sentimental, *compromised*. That he had lifted a refugee into power because she warmed his bed.

It was a cruel rumor that would spread like wildfire, however ridiculous the accusation.

Val-Theris's silence settled heavily between them, and to Jesenia, it was worse than any insult. She turned her head slowly, just enough to look at him. There was no anger in her eyes. No accusation.

Will you not speak for me?

Val-Theris lowered his gaze.

The meeting adjourned soon after. The councilors rose in a rustle of fabric and soft voices, already dissecting the exchange as they left. The council chamber emptied more slowly than Jesenia expected.

She stood near the tall windows, letting the late afternoon light wash across her shawl, watching as the men filed out in measured pairs and trios. Their voices were low but animated, already dissecting the meeting as though she had not been present at all—already rewriting the narrative in which she had merely been an inconvenience rather than a voice.

She felt smaller with every footstep that echoed away.

When the doors finally closed and the chamber fell quiet, the silence felt vast. Cold.

Val-Theris remained at the head of the table, his hands braced against the marble. Without the noise of the council, the room seemed too large even for him. The gilded sigils on the walls caught the light but offered no warmth, only the sterile glow of legacy and law.

Jesenia turned slightly toward him. She suddenly realized she had been gripping the fabric of her shawl so tightly that her fingers ached.

He looked at her then, and she saw the weariness in his eyes —deeper than just fatigue. It was the look of someone who had learned too young that every choice demanded a sacrifice. It was obvious he had no words for her. Graciously, Jesenia quietly curtseyed and whispered: "It has been an honor to serve this council, your Majesty."

The words settled between them with unexpected hurt. Val-Theris felt it in his bones—the way she ached to tell him how his council's cruelty shook her, but wouldn't raise her voice above theirs to do so.

She left the chamber soon after, her footsteps soft against the stone, her presence fading from the hall like a receding tide. Val-Theris watched her go, something restless stirring beneath his ribs.

Only when she was gone did he realize how much of the room had shifted around her.

Val-Theris finally stood to face the windows as Jesenia did, the city spread out beneath him like a constellation of restless stars. His wings drooped slightly, the faint glow along their edges dimmed by exhaustion.

Rohannes approached without sound, as he always did.

"She is an impressive girl. She held her ground," Rohannes said quietly. "They felt it."

"They will make her pay for it," Val-Theris replied.

Rohannes did not deny it. "And your silence makes it easier."

Val-Theris closed his eyes. "If I speak too loudly, I give them rumor. If I stay quiet, I abandon her. I have nowhere safe to land."

"It is a cruel place to be," Rohannes agreed. "But that is why you are king, and they are not."

Val-Theris laughed once, hollow. "I am a king because I was born a god, not because I earned the title."

Rohannes watched him for a long moment, before turning the conversation back to Lady Jesenia. "You can not protect her by pretending she isn't there. If giving her a voice destroys what balance remains in this city, at least the destruction will be honest."

Val-Theris thought back to his vision of his beloved city burning under his throne, swallowing harshly before turning to his companion with a weak smile. "Perhaps I should give you a seat in my councilor's chamber, too."

Rohannes gave him a weak smile back, and the two of them stared out beyond the window. The city shifted below them, restless and alive.

Val-Theris felt the weight of every choice pressing down upon him.

For the first time, he wondered if he had never been meant to balance might with mercy after all—but to test how much of it he was willing to lose.

JESENIA STOPPED GOING to the palace.

The decision was not dramatic. It did not arrive with resolve or bitterness. She simply…did not go. Her voice was of no use. When summons for new sessions arrived, she answered none of them. Her time was better spent in the rhythm of the quarter. She kept her hands busy. Busy meant silent. Silent meant safe. And at least here, among her people, she felt like she was making a difference.

But the city had a way of announcing its disruptions before they arrived. She felt it first as a tightening in the air, a subtle stillness that rippled through the square. When she looked up, Val-Theris stood at the mouth of the street, eyes locked on her—something between worry and frustration.

He wore no armor this time. His crimson tunic was simple, his wings drawn close behind him so they did not brush against the low stone walls. Rohannes lingered at a distance, far enough away to pretend he was not listening.

"Lady Jesenia," he said. "Your absence among the councilors has been noted."

Jesenia swallowed, and her words slipped out with the same unintended sharpness. "So it has."

"Your people require your voice."

She felt herself hold back a scoff. "I'm of better use here in the quarter where I belong, your Majesty."

Val-Theris let out an exasperated sigh. "If this is about my silence in the first meeting, it was not meant to upset you. In that chamber, I cannot seem to favor anyone. I thought the distance would make your position more credible."

"Then why invite me at all?" she snapped. "If you had no intention of listening, or letting my voice be heard, why even ask me there at all? Your silence doesn't protect me, it only gives them permission. All it did was tell me that my voice only matters when it is useful to *you*."

That struck him. She saw it in the faint tightening of his jaw, the way his gaze softened but did not waver.

"You matter," Val-Theris said. He opened his mouth as if to say something softer, but quickly shut it. "I need you there," he said. "Not because you are convenient. Not because the quarter trusts you. But because you tell me the truth when no one else will."

She held his gaze, her heartbeat an unsteady drum beneath her ribs. "Then stop letting them treat me as vermin in a chamber where my voice should be equal to theirs."

For a moment, relief flickered across his face before his composure returned.

"Yes, my lady," he agreed.

As expected, the council chamber was colder the next time Jesenia entered. It had been days, and the same distaste for her still lingered as heavy as it did the first time.

Val-Theris stood at the head of the table, his wings drawn close, his presence filling the room with restrained force.

"She stays," he said, before anyone had a chance to speak.

The words landed like a dropped gauntlet.

Of course, the objections rose quickly—measured, rehearsed. Varin spoke of precedent. Myrran spoke of unrest. Others spoke as though Jesenia were not present at all.

Jesenia waited. When Val-Theris silenced them at last, the room shifted. A line had been drawn.

One that could not be erased.

ELEVEN

Word had spread before dawn: the Angel himself was coming to tour the quarter, to see how the Lunarethians were living with his own eyes. By midmorning, the narrow streets were lined with bodies pressed close together beneath the worn archways, shoulders brushing, hands clasped tightly at sides or folded into sleeves.

Jesenia stood near the center of the square. Her hands were hidden beneath her shawl, fingers laced together to still their restless tremor. She told herself she was here only because she had been asked by Val-Theris to show him what he had not yet seen. That this was a duty of her station as a councilor at his side, and not a choice.

She knew her presence beside him would only sharpen the whispers already curling through the city like smoke. And yet, when Val-Theris had sent word at sunrise, his request had been simple: *show me where I have been blind.*

Now, as the sound of approaching armor rippled down the cobbled street, she felt the shift in the air before she saw him. The tension sharpened. Conversations died mid-breath. A child was pulled closer. Someone near the edge of the square crossed hurriedly, as though he might demand it.

Val-Theris appeared moments later, framed in gold against the rising sun.

He never wore his crown, Jesenia noticed, but his presence was far more symbolic than any golden halo above his head. He wore his gilded plate armor and a cape that barely brushed the floor with each step. The fabric was draped in a deep arc that made it easy for his wings to move freely. They were stretched loosely behind him, pale feathers brushing dust from the ground as he walked toward her.

The crowd bowed instinctively, but Jesenia noticed the division immediately.

Refugees leaned forward despite themselves, eyes bright with tentative hope, hunger and gratitude tangled together in their expressions. Solmiris's citizens near the periphery turned away, muttering their unease beneath their breath. The *Hastati* scanned every shadow with restless precision, hands tight against polished hilts, bodies already braced for disorder.

When Val-Theris reached Jesenia in the square, the noise dulled to silence in her ears.

The distance between them was closed, and the weight of his presence followed like a tide. He stopped close enough that she had to tilt her head slightly to meet his eyes—close enough that she could feel the warmth of him, the faint displacement of air as if caught in his golden aura.

"Thank you for joining me today," he said softly, his voice meant only for her.

"I wasn't sure I should," she admitted. Her voice was steadier than she felt.

"That is why I asked *you*," Val-Theris replied. Something unreadable flickered across his expression before it smoothed again. "Come."

They walked side by side through the quarter's winding streets, his guards trailing a purposeful distance behind them. Close enough to hold the fragile perimeter intact, far enough to offer the illusion of privacy. Everywhere they went, eyes followed. Hundreds of them. Layered with hunger, hope, suspicion.

Jesenia felt them like a blade against her back.

"You know what this looks like. What your people will say," she said at last, breaking the silence. She kept her gaze fixed ahead, on cracked stone and sagging doorframes and laundry lines strung too tightly between buildings.

"I do," Val-Theris said. His tone was even, unyielding. "That is the point."

"You'll make yourself a target," she murmured.

"I already am."

She hesitated, then glanced at him sidelong. In the pale light filtering through broken rooftops, his face was softer than she had ever seen it. There was exhaustion carved deep beneath his composure, an effort that never seemed to fully ease.

"You'll make me one too," Jesenia said quietly.

That made him look at her. His expression remained unreadable, but his voice softened when he spoke. "You've been one from the moment you walked through the gates."

"Is that supposed to comfort me?"

"No, but it is your reality nonetheless. Cruelty is easier to justify when there is a scapegoat to pin it on. You have become the face of your people, however much it was not your intention."

The words were nearly swallowed by the hum of the street, but they landed all the same.

The crowd thinned as they reached the old courtyard, the hush of the city breaking into fragments—the rhythm of boots on stone, the crack of wood against cobbles, a child's laughter echoing briefly before being hushed again.

Val-Theris paused beneath the partial shade of an archway, gesturing subtly for the guards to spread wider and keep the onlookers at bay. Jesenia followed, her pulse high in her throat, acutely aware of the stillness that settled between them when they stopped.

"Maybe we should stop. It's unsettling," she said softly—meaning the quarter, the attention, the weight of so many watching eyes.

"Are you afraid you'll anger your people by being seen with me?" he asked.

She turned to face him fully, fingers twisting faintly into the edge of her shawl. "Val-Theris, they're already angry. The council. Your people. My people. Everyone. Walking through this quarter is…" She drew a breath, steadying herself. "This just creates more unrest. Let me step back. You don't need me at your side to keep your promises. I've said what I have to say in our sessions."

His wings shifted behind him, pale feathers catching threads of sunlight like molten glass. "No," he said, without hesitation. "If anyone resents your presence at my side, let them. Resigning changes nothing."

Her breath caught before she could temper it, heat rising unbidden beneath her ribs. She wanted to argue, but something in his gaze stilled her.

It was conviction.

A small hand tugged suddenly at the edge of Val-Theris's wing. Jesenia startled, turning just in time to see one of the children she often cared for that must have slipped through the line. He was barefoot, dust-smudged, fearless, peering up at the king with curiosity.

"Are you an angel?" the child asked, "Or a chicken?"

Without missing a beat, Val-Theris answered solemnly, "That depends who you ask."

Jesenia laughed into her hand—a short, surprised sound she couldn't stop in time. The child grinned, delighted. The laughter drew attention, but not all of it was kind.

A guard approached moments later, bowing slightly. "My king, the citizens grow restless. Perhaps we should move on."

Val-Theris didn't look away from Jesenia's bright face when he answered. "Let them watch."

For a heartbeat, Jesenia forgot the crowd entirely. The press of eyes. The muttered voices. The weight of the city balanced on the narrow space between them. All she felt was the warmth of sunlight against her shoulders, the faint hush of his breath as he stood so close, and the gravity pulling them nearer without meaning to.

Then Val-Theris stepped back—the distance deliberate, his expression carefully schooled into composure once more.

"Show me the sick?" he suggested softly.

And Jesenia did.

By the time they returned to the square, the tension had only deepened. Imperial citizens whispered sharply from the edges of the crowd, resentment sharpened by fear and pride. Refugees lingered nearby with careful gratitude in their eyes, as though afraid to hope too openly.

As Val-Theris mounted the low steps near the fountain, Jesenia caught the hard glances exchanged among his guards in her direction.

Silent warnings, unspoken but unmistakable.

TWELVE

Val-Theris sat at the head of the long table, wings folded close behind him, every line of his posture carefully composed. His expression was serene to the point of artifice—an angel carved from patience and restraint. Those who knew him well could see the tension in the set of his shoulders, the way his fingers rested too firmly against the arm of his chair.

Jesenia sat in her assigned chair at his right. She promised herself that she would brave the council again for the sake of her people, but she kept her presence small. Still, she could feel the weight of the room pressing against her ribs.

Lunareth was being discussed, but only to the degree that painted her people as a plague, and not as war-ravaged victims of a fight they had no part in.

The doors of the council hall swung open, and the warmth of fire and the scent of ash swept into the room. It went quiet with confusion for a moment, and when Jesenia looked to the gilded doors, she saw a sight that made her sick.

It was the man who cruelly killed her brother as she watched helplessly. The man who stole her last living relative.

He wore deep obsidian armor, darkened with evil and death to the point that it would never shine again. His gray cloak smoldered faintly at the edges, embers clinging to its hem like stubborn memories. His wings—broader and heavier than Val-Theris's—flared once, flaming viciously, before folding back against his shoulders.

"My *dear* brother," he drawled, his voice rich with amusement. "I was beginning to think Seraveth no longer had the courtesy to answer summons from its kin. Why have you ignored my letters?"

A murmur rippled through the council.

Val-Theris rose slowly from his seat. "We answer diplomacy, not bloodshed," he said evenly, "Why are you here, Val-Oros?"

Jesenia ceased breathing. All of the truths she had known came rushing to her in an instant, and sickly realized that the reason she did not recognize Val-Oros during the attack was because the fires of her home burning hid the flaming wings that protruded from his back. The timbre of his voice—that cruel, almost playful lilt—was seared into her memory. She heard it layered over the crackle of flames, over the screams of her village, over the wet sound of her brother's body hitting the dirt. She moved her hands into her lap to hide the shaking, begging herself not to cry.

"To offer you mercy," Val-Oros replied lightly, as though discussing trade routes rather than war. His smile was sharp as a blade's edge. "Before your stubbornness forces my hand once again."

He paced a few steps into the chamber, boots echoing softly against marble. Then, he took one heavy step onto the table that stretched the length of the room between the councilors. "Korvath grows weary of Seraveth's interference of my business in Lunareth. Withdraw your legions, or I will return to the border."

His eyes gleamed with wickedness. "And I will not stop at the border next time."

"What *business* in Lunareth?" Val-Theris asked. "You reduced their homes to ash. If there is anything of Lunareth left, you will not find it in the land."

Val-Oros's gaze snapped to Jesenia's dark hair, standing out amongst the white and gold of the chamber, despite her attempts to shrink into herself. Recognition flared in his eyes, cruel, sharp, and delighted.

"Well," he said softly, turning fully toward her. "What do we have here?" He took a step closer, eyes gleaming. "One of your refugees, brother? This meek little dove sheltered beneath your wing?"

Val-Oros approached her from his risen position on the table in a predatory way, his presence radiating heat. "I remember you," he said, almost gently. "The girl who trembled as I smashed that foolish boy's face in." When Jesenia's lip quivered slightly, his smile widened. But Jesenia was careful not to cry out. She sat frozen, shaking, lips pressed together until they blanched. She would not give Val-Oros the satisfaction. He kneeled to be closer.

"No tears?" he murmured. "Has the pacifist learned indifference? Or perhaps my brother has taught you that compassion is a luxury best burned away."

A faint, broken sound escaped her throat—no more than a breath caught between grief and fury.

"I often wonder if the bleeding took him first, or the fire." He hummed as if it was a question worth contemplating, and then a crack split the air between them, shifting Val-Oros's and Jesenia's gaze to the King of Seraveth.

Val-Theris's hand had twitched against the table; the marble beneath it fractured, spider-webbing outward. His wings shuddered, feathers vibrating with barely restrained violence.

Rohannes, standing at his side, gave the smallest shake of his head.

Not here. Not now.

"Enough," Val-Theris said. His voice was quiet. Even. The restraint cost him blood that pooled at his broken fingertips. "This hall is for diplomacy, not torment."

Val-Oros straightened, amused. "Ah, but torment *is* diplomacy." He turned his attention to the council, spreading his hands. "It is how the world remembers who commands and who kneels."

Then he paused. His gaze drifted back to Jesenia. Something in his expression changed, and he roughly grabbed her hand from her lap, lacing their fingers together. His eyes glazed over into a milky white as his prophetic sight took hold.

For a heartbeat, the world seemed to hold its breath.

Val-Oros saw her. He saw gold turned to ash. A city fractured by its own fear. He saw his brother kneeling in ruin, and at the center of it all, this woman in a devastatingly pivotal heap, crumbled lifeless to the ground.

The vision vanished as quickly as it came. Val-Oros smiled.

"You will be this kingdom's undoing," he said lightly, turning back to the council. "*Mark my words.*"

The chamber went still.

Val-Theris's head snapped up in warning, severing the contact between the two and shoving his brother from his spot atop the table. "Val-Oros, enough."

But he only shrugged. "Withdraw from Lunareth. If you do not, Korvath's flames will make this gilded palace the next pyre." He met his brother's gaze, eyes alight with cruel certainty. A challenge.

Silence thickened, heavy as smoke. Val-Theris inclined his head once, the motion precise and cold. "Then let Korvath remember *this* mercy, brother, because when I answer your flames, there will be none."

Val-Oros laughed—a merciless sound—and turned for the doors, his burning wings casting a red glow across the marble as he left.

The council was dismissed then quickly ushered out of the chamber for an intermission, leaving Jesenia alone with Val-Theris and Rohannes. When she was finally away from the judging eyes of the council, she tried standing from her seat, but sank back into the cushion and wept.

Val-Theris reached for her instantly, wings open as if to shield her from eyes that were not there. His golden-kissed feathers trembled with the effort it took not to chase Val-Oros back to Korvath and leave his ruins in the dirt.

"Why didn't you tell me?" His voice was low, rough. "That it was him?"

"I didn't realize until…" Jesenia said through her tears. "It doesn't matter. It wouldn't have changed anything. Everything I cared about was lost long before you could have helped."

"I still could have tried." The words shattered his fury into helplessness. "I cannot listen to him taunt you that way," he whispered. "And do *nothing*."

"You did the right thing," she said softly.

He pressed his forehead to the edge of the marble table, breath uneven. "I want to kill him."

"I know," she whispered. "And I cannot say I understand, but please, whatever you do, don't do it in Lunareth's name."

He looked at her then, his heart pounding in his ears. He understood what she meant: *don't make her or her people a martyr against the cruelty of this war.*

The silence that followed was not of Val-Theris's acceptance, but now was not the time to discuss it further. The three of them stayed in the chamber for a moment longer until Jesenia's tears dried against the lingering echo of Val-Oros's presence. The chamber had dimmed from the afternoon sun when Jesenia stood.

There was still a tremor in the Angel-King's feathers, but he stood with her. She made a step as if to leave the room, but stopped suddenly and turned her attention back to Val-Theris.

"What did he mean?" she asked quietly. It was careful in the way of someone who already suspected the answer might hurt. "When he said I would undo this kingdom," she clarified. "That wasn't his cruelty alone. He meant it."

Val-Theris's jaw tightened. His gaze shifted, just briefly, to the marble floor between them.

"Val-Oros does not speak without intention," he said at last.

Jesenia felt the weight in his words immediately. "So he saw something."

"Yes."

Her breath caught. "And you won't tell me what."

"I can't," Val-Theris said.

Jesenia searched his face, her expression torn between fear and disbelief. "You see the future too," she said. "If he saw this country's ruin, wouldn't you know it too?"

Val-Theris exhaled slowly, as though steadying himself against a painful admission.

"Our gifts are not the same," he said quietly. "My brother's sight is…narrower. More precise. He sees *people*. When he touches someone whose existence bends the path of what is to come, the vision comes unbidden."

"And you?" she asked.

Val-Theris hesitated. "I see fragments," he said. "Symbols. Echoes. I am given the *shape* of endings, not their names. I see faceless people, but the setting is clear. I can see suffering, but not far enough to understand the source."

Jesenia absorbed that in silence, her fingers curling faintly into the fabric at his chest.

"So if he knows what he saw," she said slowly, "then he is the only one who can tell us what it means."

"Precisely. And he would never. He would rather let fear do the work for him. He said just enough to give credibility to the council's fears of you and your people. He is attempting to undermine me with a civil fracture."

Jesenia looked away then, her gaze drifting down the long corridor, as though she half-expected Val-Oros to step back through the shadows and finish what he had started.

"Do you believe him?" she asked softly.

Val-Theris closed his eyes, because the answer was simply: yes. He knew better than to distrust prophecy, and behind his eyes, he remembered his own visions of ruin. He saw Jesenia as Val-Oros had long before he knew her name.

But he did not say any of it. Instead, he opened his eyes and met her gaze.

"I believe that Val-Oros mistakes cause for blame," he said carefully.

Her brow furrowed. "Meaning?"

"Meaning that the future he saw may not exist *because* of you," Val-Theris said. "But because of what others choose to do in response to you."

Jesenia studied him for a long moment, as though weighing the truth of that against the fear coiling in her chest.

"And you?" she asked again. "What have *you* seen?"

The question was softer now, but Val-Theris felt the answer press against his ribs, insistent and sharp.

You.

He swallowed. "I have seen many things," he said instead. "Enough to know that prophecy is a warning, but that it can also be prepared for."

She did not look entirely convinced, but she nodded, accepting what he was willing to give her.

"For what it's worth," Jesenia said after a moment, her voice steady, "I never wanted to be anyone's undoing."

"Nor are you," he said softly. "The failure of this kingdom will never be on the shoulders of you or your people. That burden is mine."

He wanted to say more, to admit to the things he saw before she arrived at his gates, but knew it would do nothing but weigh her down with guilt that was not hers to bear. He knew this much, even if he would never say it aloud: some endings did not arrive because they were chosen, but because courage and the strength of a people existed where power could not tolerate it.

THIRTEEN

With the unexpected interruption, the council had run well into the night, the sun long since hidden behind the horizon when they adjourned. Jesenia's heart had been heavy of late, and she disappeared into the quiet gardens of the palace with a piece of parchment she had taken from the chamber.

She approached a fountain at the center of the garden, and folded the paper meticulously against the stone edge until it created the shape of a bowl, meant to be used in place of a lantern. She plucked a flower from the beds near her knees and placed it in the paper.

She had no fire to light it, but it wasn't as important as letting the lantern float freely in the water, even if it had nowhere to go but in circles in the fountain.

Jesenia had intended to release the lantern and leave, but her heart began to weep as she whispered her brother's name into the night. She hadn't expected anyone to notice her here as she murmured soft fragments of Lunarethian river songs beneath her breath.

"Do you mourn?"

The voice was low, deep, and resonated in her chest. Val-Theris stood a few paces away, moonlight soft across his pale features, his wings folded close and shadowed behind him.

"I'm sorry. I didn't mean to trespass in your garden," she said shamefully. "I will leave."

Val-Theris didn't seem to mind her presence though, coming closer and kneeling next to her before she tried to stand.

"Is this a Lunarethian tradition?" he asked, gently running his fingers along the delicate paper.

Jesenia nodded and her gaze fell back to the crude lantern. "My people send light to the river when someone passes. Today made me realize I never got the chance to properly mourn my brother, and I can only hope that the earth has been kind to his remains."

He regarded her for a long moment, the silence stretching delicate and thin between them. He had no words of comfort to offer her—none that mattered anyway. It was his war with his own brother that took hers from her life.

Jesenia bowed her head, tears slipping silently down the curve of her cheeks and the lines of her jaw. After a long while, Val-Theris pulled a sheet of parchment from his coat pocket. An unimportant piece of paper that was from an earlier summons. He gently presented it to her.

"Would you teach me how to fold it into a lantern?" he asked gently, as if he was asking her for the world.

Jesenia blinked, but took it from his hand and folded it with the same care as before. She handed it back to him. He looked around for an offering before pulling a loose feather from his own wing. He set it delicately into the lantern and then pushed it into the water.

"For all those that Lunareth has lost," he said mournfully. He had meant it sincerely, and Jesenia felt it in her soul. It caused her tears to fall harder.

The moment passed. Neither of them moved closer, and yet the space between them felt smaller somehow.

"I did not mean for you to see me weep," Jesenia said softly, her eyes lowered. "It is not becoming of someone who claims to speak for her people."

Val-Theris glanced at her, his blond hair catching the moonlight. "It is becoming of someone who carries the strength of her people alone."

She did not have an answer for that. It felt like an eternity before Jesenia found the strength to stand again. He stood with her, helping her to her feet with gentle ease.

"Thank you, Val-Theris, for mourning with me," she said. A beat passed, and she looked up to watch an owl swoop over their heads and land in one of the well-trimmed trees of the garden. "It's peaceful here," she murmured. "I've almost forgotten what pain lies in the city on the other side of these walls."

She began walking, following the stone path through the flower beds. Her fingers brushed the soft leaves of roses and the vines that fell from the balconies above them. Val-Theris walked at her side.

"That is the purpose of this place," he replied. "It was built to be a fortress of calm and beauty amid chaos and war."

"Fortress?" She smiled faintly. "That's the difference between us. You make it sound like a prison with flowers, where I see a garden."

They fell into comfortable silence for a time, the soft rhythm of their steps filling the space between them. Jesenia's hand trailed across a low hedge of lilies.

"Do you ever think of what comes after?" she asked suddenly. "When the war with Korvath ends. When I return home with my people. When peace is no longer something you chase?"

He glanced at her, curious. "What do you mean?"

She shrugged. "What do you think life might look like then? For me, for my people. For you."

Val-Theris considered this. "I've never thought of an after," he said quietly. "Only of the next crisis. My life is a chain of moments spent averting disasters that have not yet happened."

"That sounds exhausting."

"It is, but it leaves little room for imagination."

She looked down, thoughtful, and then, so softly he almost didn't hear her, she said: "I'd like a family one day. A large one. As many children as my body will carry."

Val-Theris stopped walking. The image that rose in his mind startled him: Jesenia surrounded by sunlight and laughter, her hands gentle and her womb full, the world unbroken. He couldn't remember the last time he'd pictured something so simple.

"You would make a good mother," he said sincerely.

She turned to him with a gentle smile. "Do angels dream of families?"

He hesitated. The question was innocent, but something about it lodged deep in him. "I don't know if I can," he said at last. "In any sense that matters."

Her brow furrowed. "You mean you don't want to?"

"No." He exhaled slowly. "I mean I'm not certain it's even possible. My brother has taken many wives, but none have given him children. I've never...*tried*," he cleared his throat, "but I suspect the same curse binds me." Jesenia's expression softened. "It appears to be a flaw of godhood. We were not made to create life. Only to preserve or destroy it. The Light gave us its power, but not its gift. Perhaps it feared what we might become if we learned how to love as mortals do."

The silence stretched between them, filled with the sound of wind through the vines. Jesenia reached for a blossom and twisted it gently from the stem. "Then perhaps that's why it made mortals," she said. "To remind you what it looks like."

Val-Theris smiled faintly, though his eyes were far away. "I could never forget."

She tucked the flower behind her ear and started walking again, as though the conversation were over, light as a passing breeze. But when she glanced back, she found him still standing where she'd left him, staring at her as though trying to see the shape of a future he only just now realized he would never have.

He finally caught up to her after a moment.

"Have you eaten?" Val-Theris said softly from behind her. "The council ran late, you would have missed the ration line."

"Not today, no. How can I eat when my people starve?"

"How can you speak for them if you grow so malnourished you can't stand?" He stepped beside her, hands braced against a cold stone railing, close enough that she felt the faint warmth radiating from him. "I would invite you to dinner, but I suspect you'll reject me."

He paused slightly at the implication of that, as if it was a way of courting her as opposed to a courtesy. She didn't seem to feel the same way. She sighed softly.

"I can't, Val-Theris. Not until I can negotiate better conditions for my people."

"Having your first meal of the day is not a sin, Jesenia."

For a long moment, neither of them spoke, letting the city breathe below them, letting the weight of their choices sit between them. Val-Theris wanted to offer more, would have even gone without a meal himself if only she would eat, but she wouldn't, and he knew it.

She shook her head once more. "I can't have my people hate me as much as yours do."

His head turned slightly, pale eyes catching hers. "Your people could never hate you, and mine don't know you."

Her throat tightened. "And you do?"

Val-Theris's jaw shifted. "Better than I should," he said, his voice roughened.

She turned toward him, her shawl brushing lightly against his arm, and the air sharpened instantly—the heat of proximity too molten to ignore.

He reached for her hand, and she let him. His thumb traced small circles against her knuckles, his gaze locked on hers like he was memorizing her face. Then, he placed a chaste kiss to her hand before pressing her palm gently to his chest over the steady, thunderous beat of his heart.

"I cannot promise we will convince the others in the council to share our cause, but by my heart, Lady Jesenia, I swear to you I will do what I can for Lunareth."

She felt in the weight of his words that he meant more than just a promise that her people would eat, but knew there was so much he was unable to say.

FOURTEEN

JESENIA STOOD NEAR THE PLAZA, her arms full of freshly cleaned folded linens, when a sound rolled down the narrow streets. It was a jagged, uneven roar that split into fragments she couldn't yet make out. Then came the pounding of boots against cobblestone, the rush of bodies pressing into one another, voices rising sharp and panicked into the cool air.

She dropped the linens without thinking, weaving through the cluster of people until the street opened into a corridor of chaos.

It was worry over grain rations. The commotion always began with food.

Dozens of Solmiris's citizens surged against the low market walls, their anger loud and sharp as they shouted accusations at the refugees clustered defensively near the steps. Someone had screamed *thief*, and the word caught like fire in hay. Stones clattered against the worn brick, children cried, and hands gripped whatever they could find to hold as weapons.

And then the banners appeared—crimson and ivory, the

Hastati moving in formation, halberds catching the weak sunlight. Val-Theris was with them.

He walked ahead of the line of soldiers, pale wings drawn wide, his presence like thunder rolling into the storm. The sound of him moving through the crowd wasn't just command, it was gravity, pulling everything into stillness as he passed.

The citizens fell back in restless murmurs, some lowering their fists, others shifting uneasily but refusing to yield. Jesenia saw the soldiers form a shielded line at the base of the steps, keeping the two groups apart, the hum of tension vibrating sharp beneath the quiet.

One of the merchants spat toward the ground at Val-Theris's feet.

"Protecting them again," the man said, his voice rough, bitter. Val-Theris's head lifted, his gaze steady and unyielding as he turned to face the man directly. A soldier stepped forward to detain the man, but the king stopped him with a raised hand.

"We are one people within these walls," he said, his voice calm but edged in steel, carrying easily through the square.

The merchant's jaw tightened, but he said nothing more.

Behind the wall of guards, Jesenia pushed her way forward, her shawl clutched tightly around her shoulders. She'd thought—foolishly, perhaps—that staying quiet would keep her unseen, but the closer she came to the king, the louder the whispers, darting like embers through the crowd.

Lunarethians spoke with awe: *That's her. The Angel's voice. She walks the palace halls.*

And then, sharper from the Imperial edge of the square: *The foreigner. She speaks in his ear. This is her doing.*

Heat prickled against Jesenia's skin, her pulse rising beneath the weight of too many eyes. She wanted to melt back into shadow, but Val-Theris's gaze had already found her, and that single look only spurred the unrest forward.

The riot didn't break. The air remained sharp and dangerous, the threat of violence lingering above them all. The guards began dispersing citizens in either direction, separating Imperial-born from refugees, voices hard and clipped as they forced distance.

"Get her out of here," Val-Theris murmured low but firm to Rohannes. The words reached Jesenia across the space between them, and for a heartbeat, she froze.

Rohannes approached, gesturing her toward the palace gates beyond the plaza, but she shook her head, her voice breaking out sharper than she intended.

"I'm not leaving them."

Rohannes glanced toward Val-Theris for confirmation. He met Jesenia's eyes for a measured moment before giving a single small nod. He had more important things to worry about, and Jesenia knew this argument was not worth the time. The rise of clashing voices already swallowed them both whole, and bodies pressed against bodies separated them in the narrow streets.

Solmiris's citizens shoved against refugee barricades, steel and wood slamming against makeshift shields, voices sharp with fear and hatred. Jesenia moved through the chaos with her shawl drawn tight, weaving between frightened children and screaming mothers, shouting until her voice was raw, trying to pull her people back from the fray.

"Stop—please, stop!" she begged, her words nearly swallowed by the roar of the crowd. "This isn't the way!"

But no one was listening anymore, too caught up in their own hatred to care about anything else.

A heavy stone struck the wall beside her, splintering in a spray of dust. The second hit closer, clipping the edge of her shoulder, sending her stumbling into the crush of bodies as pain shot sharp down her arm.

Jesenia gasped, forcing herself upright, but before she could retreat, someone shoved her hard from behind. It was likely an accident, but with so many people in the streets, the force pushed her to her knees. Her joints scraped the cobblestone ground as she fell, the heat of the crowd pressing in until she could barely breathe.

For a moment, everything blurred—the rocks, the noise, the bodies surging and shouting around her. It was just like the chaos when Lunareth fell, only worse this time, for her people would have nowhere to go if they were abandoned.

Her vision swam as she pulled herself up onto her hands, her breath ragged, the sting of her scraped palms mixing with the sharp ache radiating down her shoulder.

The *Hastati* forced their way through the chaos, halberds raised, gold armor flashing in the sun as they drove the crowd back in a wall of steel and force. Shouts turned to screams as bodies pressed against each other, the narrow street dissolving into violence.

"Clear the square! Now!" Rohannes roared, his voice cutting through the square.

A familiar voice followed, deeper, sharper, closer: "Jesenia!"

She turned her head sharply, vision swimming. Val-Theris moved like a blade through the chaos, his pale wings spread wide, sunlight catching along the ivory curve of each feather as he forced his way toward her. His soldiers formed a line at his back, cutting a clean path through the still dense but scattering crowd, but his focus never wavered from her.

He reached her in a rush, dropping to one knee, his hand cupping her cheek immediately as his gaze scanned the shallow cut blooming red against her temple and the bruise at her cheek that she only just realized was there.

Val-Theris breathed heavy, and though his voice was soft, there was something wild beneath it, a tremor he couldn't disguise. "Are you hurt anywhere else?"

"I'm fine," she rasped, her voice rough from shouting, her breath uneven. "It's nothing."

He tilted her chin gently, his thumb brushing the edge of blood near her hairline, his jaw tightening. "This is not nothing."

"I was only trying to—"

"You were in the middle of a riot," Val-Theris said, his voice rising sharper than he intended before softening again, ragged and low. "You could have been trampled. Killed."

His wings curved around them instinctively, creating a fragile shield from the chaos still unfolding in the square, the soft sweep of feathers brushing against her back as if to anchor her in his orbit.

"Why are they doing this?" Jesenia whispered finally, her throat tight as she steadied herself with one hand against his arm. "Why can't they see this isn't us?"

Val-Theris's gaze lifted beyond her, scanning the street, the scattered remnants of overturned carts and broken glass and stones.

"They do see," he said softly, his voice carrying something quiet and terrible beneath it. "They just don't care."

He rose, pulling Jesenia carefully to her feet, steadying her when her balance faltered. His hand lingered against her waist as he turned sharply to the Angelicus Prime, his voice carrying steel now.

"Lock down the quarter," he ordered. Then, louder, so the lingering crowd could hear: "You're all under curfew. Anyone out after dark will be detained until morning."

Rohannes and what loyal men followed bowed sharply and vanished into the chaos, shouting commands as they pushed the last stragglers out of the square.

When Val-Theris turned back to her, his expression was stripped raw beneath the rigid control. His thumb brushed faintly along her cheek again, his voice quieter now, almost breaking around the edges.

"Let me help you. Please," he whispered, the words pulled from somewhere deeper than his throat.

Jesenia blinked, startled by the weight of them, her throat aching as she searched his face. "Okay," she said softly, though even she didn't believe it would help the situation to receive his care.

Val-Theris exhaled slowly, his jaw tightening faintly as his gaze dropped to where blood had dried against her temple. With a hand on the small of her back, and his wings shielding most of her body, he led her back up through the terraces and into his citadel.

Despite the opulence of the structure, the palace walls felt smaller than they had ever been.

Val-Theris gave her a room of her own, and commanded her to sit on the plush bed. Her shawl fell to the quilt, and she didn't have the strength to pull it back over her shoulders. Her scraped palms still stung faintly where bits of stone and dirt clung to the wounds.

Outside her chamber windows, the city murmured like a restless beast—distant shouts and muffled cries drifting faintly upward toward them, never allowing them to forget what lingered there.

She hadn't spoken since she arrived. Not when the healer wrapped her shoulder and cleaned her hands. Not when the servants offered her hot soup. Val-Theris stood in the corner, his wings furled tightly behind him as though holding himself together by force.

"They hate us," Jesenia whispered when they were alone once more, her hands clutching the folds of her skirt until the fabric wrinkled beneath her grip.

Val-Theris turned sharply from the window, his jaw tense, but he didn't interrupt.

"They don't even see us as people," she continued, her voice raw, small in the quiet room. "We're just…thieves. Liars. Strangers in their city. And no matter what we do, no matter how quiet we try to be, how careful, how grateful, it will never be enough."

Her words cracked on the last breath, shattering against the heavy silence. She dropped her face into her hands, shoulders curling inward, trembling hard enough that her scraped palms pressed painfully against her skin.

Val-Theris crossed the room in three strides and lowered himself onto the bed beside her, silent, steady, his presence grounding even before his touch reached her.

"This is my fault," he said, his voice low and rough around the edges.

"No—"

"Yes," Val-Theris said softly, cutting across her protest without force, only certainty. "I should have seen this coming. I should have stopped it before it reached this point."

"You can't stop a city from hating, Val-Theris," she whispered, her voice breaking despite her effort to hold it steady.

"I should have *tried* harder," he murmured, his gaze fixed on the floor. "I put you in their sights when I defended you. I gave them a name, a face, a reason to sharpen their blades."

Val-Theris's jaw clenched, his hands tightening into fists on his knees before he exhaled slowly, forcing himself to loosen them.

Then Jesenia's composure finally broke. The sobs came slow at first, muffled against the soft fabric wrapping her hands, but when they deepened, Val-Theris moved without hesitation. He slid his arm around her shoulders, drawing her gently against his chest, his other hand cradling the back of her head as he leaned forward until his forehead brushed her temple.

"Breathe," he murmured softly, his voice low, patient, steadying. "It's okay. You're safe now."

She wanted to believe him.

Minutes bled into hours, her tears soaking through his tunic, her small tremors easing only gradually as exhaustion dulled the edges of her fear. At some point, Val-Theris shifted, settling them more fully onto the bed, keeping her close as though the act itself could shield her from the entire weight of the city outside.

When she finally fell asleep, breath warm and uneven against his chest, Val-Theris lowered himself back against the headboard, his gaze fixed on the ceiling above them.

He didn't sleep.

Instead, he unfurled his wings, pale and endless, and curved them carefully around them both, closing them off from the world.

Outside, Solmiris's tension sparked like logs in a hearth. Inside, she slept soundly, perhaps for the first time since she arrived in his city.

And Val-Theris sat awake in the dark, holding her, his thumb stroking the edge of her sleeve absently—memorizing the warmth of her, knowing that when he left that room, backlash would come swift and cold.

"You *humiliate* this council!" Varin spat, his voice rising above the others. "Every time you parade that foreign girl at your side, you tell this city that its people matter less than hers. Our citizens will not forget this!"

"She has nothing to do with yesterday's unrest," Val-Theris said evenly, his voice immovable. It was a farce though, and he knew it. He had spent the night at her side, and he made no effort to hide it from anyone. It was a mistake he knew he would pay for, but no longer had the patience to care.

"She has everything to do with it!" another councilor snapped, slamming his hand against the carved table. "You feed them, you house them, you walk their streets—and you do it all with *her*! They see her as your envoy, your chosen voice, and your citizens resent it. If you keep aligning yourself with her, Solmiris will fall just like the filth of Lunareth! And unlike those vagrants, Seraveth has no walls to turn to when ours crumble."

Val-Theris stood up suddenly, his chair scraping sharply against the floors, pale wings drawn tight to his frame, his shadow stretching long across the room.

For a moment, no one spoke. The braziers along the walls guttered, their flames bending inward as if drawn toward the king. His wings were no longer relaxed at his back; they pulled tight, feathers overlapping with a particular rigidity, as though bracing for impact.

He did not shout. That was the unsettling part.

Val-Theris's hands rested on the table now, fingers splayed against the carved stone. The marble beneath them creaked faintly, protesting the pressure. His gaze moved slowly across the councilors in a way that suggested his restraint was deliberately *chosen* as a mercy, not forced.

His voice carried without effort. It did not rise, yet it pressed outward, filling the chamber until even the smallest breath felt too loud. "If Solmiris falls, it will not be because I walked among the starving, it will be because those entrusted with its future chose cruelty over patience."

The silence that followed was absolute. No one dared interrupt him, but Val-Theris could see it in their faces that they cared not for his truth. He drew a slow breath, visibly reigning himself back in, the faint glow along his wings dimming as control reasserted itself. When he spoke again, his voice was calmer—but no less final.

"You will not use Lady Jesenia or the Lunarethian refugees as a scapegoat for your failures," he said. "And you will not threaten my kingdom with the consequences of your own unwillingness to govern our people with their best interests in mind." His gaze hardened. "Not while I still wear this crown. Not while murals of my father paint these halls. And not while it is by *my* rule you do not live as the Korvathians do under my brother. You have all grown complacent in your service to me, and I will hear no more of your baseless fears of pacifist refugees. You govern *everyone* within my walls, or none at all."

He remained standing long after the words settled, and the distance between king and council was suddenly vast.

MOONLIGHT SPILLED across the polished stone floors, silver threads glinting between pools of shadow where the torches had burned low. Jesenia's soft shoes made no sound as she slipped through the long corridor, her shawl drawn close around her shoulders, the weight of her decision pressing heavily against her chest.

She couldn't stay in the palace any longer, and she certainly couldn't risk appearing closer to Val-Theris.

Not after the shouting, the riots, the whispers cutting like shards of glass through the square. Her presence was making things worse. For him. For her people. For everyone. If she left quietly, without a word, perhaps she could still disappear into the quarter again. Become no one.

She rounded the corner into the shadowed side hall that led toward the servants' gate—and stopped dead. Val-Theris was already there.

He stood beneath one of the tall windows, where moonlight spilled across the marble, his wings half-furled. His arms were folded loosely, but there was nothing casual in his posture; he'd been waiting for her.

"Lady Jesenia."

The sound of her name on his tongue made her throat tighten, sharp and aching, but she forced her voice steady as she drew her shawl tighter around her.

"You shouldn't be awake," she said softly.

"Neither should you," Val-Theris replied, his tone quiet but edged with something deeper. "Where were you going?"

Her grip on the shawl tightened until the fabric bit into her aching palms. "To the refugee quarter where I belong."

His gaze sharpened faintly, though his voice remained soft, restrained. "You belong *here*, Jesenia, in these halls. As much as any of us."

"No," she whispered, shaking her head. "I don't. And I never will."

He stepped forward then until he stood close enough that she had to tilt her head slightly to meet his eyes.

"You think leaving will protect your people," he said quietly, his voice low and steady, as if he'd pulled the thought directly from her chest. "That if you step back into the shadows, mine will stop whispering your name." Her jaw clenched, but she didn't answer. "They won't," Val-Theris continued, softer now. "They will only sharpen the blade they've already drawn, and blame you for being too weak to fight it."

Jesenia closed her eyes briefly, forcing breath into her lungs. "You've seen how they look at me, Val-Theris. How they speak when they think I can't hear. I'm not one of you. And every time you call me into that chamber, every time you walk beside me in the quarter, you make me something I never wanted to be."

"What is that?" he asked softly.

"A symbol," she whispered. "And symbols burn."

The silence stretched between them, taut and fragile, as Val-Theris's jaw tightened faintly, shadows cutting sharp across the lines of his face.

"I didn't ask for any of this," Jesenia said finally, her voice trembling before she forced it steady. "I didn't ask for your favor, or your protection, or for people to hate me for standing beside you. My people don't need a voice in your halls, they need safety. They need to survive. And if my leaving spares them…" Her throat closed briefly, and she swallowed hard before finishing, "…then I will go."

Something flickered in his expression before he closed the distance between them fully.

"You are not leaving."

The words were soft, but there was steel beneath them, quiet and unyielding.

Jesenia lifted her chin, meeting his gaze despite the sudden rush of heat in her chest. "You don't get to decide where I belong."

His wings shifted behind him, pale feathers brushing faint motes of light from the air. When he spoke again, his voice was lower, rougher, like something held tightly beneath restraint: "I know." A pause, heavy enough to carry meaning she couldn't name. "But I can't watch you walk away."

Val-Theris's hand lifted, slow, hesitant, his fingertips hovering just shy of her bruised cheek—close enough that she could feel the faint heat radiating from his skin. But he didn't touch her fully, he simply felt a loose strand of her hair between his calloused fingers.

Jesenia couldn't move, couldn't breathe, caught in the fragile stillness between the impulse to step back and the pull to move closer.

"I will not force you to stay," Val-Theris said softly, his voice careful and composed, though his breath came slower than before. She knew he meant for more than just a bed in his home, but she also knew he would not admit it.

Jesenia nodded once, unable to trust her voice, and stepped around him. She didn't look back. She couldn't.

The next time they saw each other, Val-Theris found her near the plaza overlooking the city, her shawl pulled tightly around her shoulders against the rising wind.

"You missed the evening session," he said quietly.

"I know," Jesenia said softly, her gaze fixed on the lights scattered across the lower district. When he did not move on, she added: "I told you I would not be there."

"Jesenia."

Her name carried weight, his voice soft but unrelenting, and she finally turned to face him, forcing her expression into something steady despite the heat pooling behind her ribs.

"You know as well as I do that it's better if I don't attend the council sessions anymore."

Val-Theris stilled. His wings shifted faintly behind him, pale feathers catching the fractured moonlight. "So you will just let them win?"

"They don't *want* me there, Val-Theris," Jesenia murmured. "And I...I don't want to make things harder for you than I already have."

His jaw tightened, his silence heavier than any accusation. His eyes held hers, searching, as though there was something in her refusal to yield that unsettled him more than any battle could. Her breath caught, just faintly, and she turned away before the sound could betray her. "You have a kingdom to lead, Val-Theris. A kingdom that is not my home."

He stepped closer then, but stopped himself when he remembered they were in public, under the scrutinizing gaze of their people.

"You will not leave," he said softly, but there was steel beneath the quiet. "I will not have you hiding in the dark while they tighten the noose around us both."

Jesenia shook her head, pulling the shawl tighter around herself, the words breaking from her lips like glass under strain:

"This isn't about us."

"It is," Val-Theris said, his voice rougher now, though still quiet.

"That's what they want," she said softly. "For you to choose me. To let them call it obsession. To let them turn your people against you. And when they do, it won't just be me who pays for it, but all that remains of Lunareth's people."

"I don't care what they call it."

Her breath caught; her hands stilled in the folds of her shawl.

"You should," she whispered. "I can't stay at your side," Jesenia breathed, though her voice faltered, betraying the ache beneath her words. "I can't make my people pay the price for what I—" She broke off sharply, catching herself, forcing the thought to fracture before it could leave her tongue.

"For what you what?" he asked. "For what you *what*, Jesenia?"

Her lips parted, but no answer came. Val-Theris's hand lifted, slow and uncertain, stopping just shy of touching her cheek—so close that the faint warmth of his skin brushed against hers like ghosted heat. Neither of them moved. Neither of them breathed.

It was the closest they'd ever been to breaking.

Then, he lowered his hand, forcing his composure back into place as though it burned him to hold it.

His voice, when it came, was quiet. "You resign then."

"I do," Jesenia whispered, her chest tightening with the ache of it.

The tension hung between them like the moment before lightning breaks the sky.

Then Jesenia stepped past him without another word, her shawl trailing faintly in the sunlight as the low wind caught against the sweep of his wings.

He didn't follow.

But she felt his gaze on her back until she vanished into the quarter.

FIFTEEN

The bells rang across Seraveth at midday, summoning the city to the central plaza.

Jesenia stood at the edge of the steps leading to the assembly, her shawl drawn close against the pale light, the noise of the crowd folding around her like a restless tide. Everyone within the walls of Solmiris was called to the plaza for an announcement by the king. As much as she wanted to hide or sink into the shadows of the crowd, she knew Val-Theris's eyes would find her.

Despite her presence bringing him grief from his councilors and his people, she joined the refugees in the plaza. The unrest between the citizens and the foreigners simmered hotly between bodies, but graciously both sides kept to themselves.

Banners of crimson and ivory swayed faintly in the dry breeze, the carved marble platform at the top of the steps leading to the upper terraces glowing beneath the harsh sun. Jesenia could feel the judgmental eyes of the council watching her from behind Val-Theris.

He stood on the platform, his wings half-furled behind him, pale feathers catching the sun like fractured glass.

"We are one city," he said, his voice calm but carrying, washing over the restless crowd below. "Our walls hold us together, our blood runs together, and our survival depends on our unity."

Murmurs rolled through the plaza, harsh and uneven, the old wounds refusing to close. Jesenia caught a flicker of movement near the western archway, and something cold slid beneath her skin. And then she saw a glint of metal just a few people over, half-hidden beneath a sleeve, sunlight flashing briefly against the edge of steel.

Her breath stopped.

"Val-Theris!" she shouted, knowing that he would hear her, at least enough to heighten his attention to the people around him. Her body followed her voice, lunging in the direction of the figure with the dagger.

The sound of the crowd fractured in an instant, gasps swallowed by chaos as Val-Theris turned sharply, wings flaring wide as the blade clanged harmlessly against polished armor inches from his exposed neck, missing its target only because Jesenia managed to shove her body into the assassin's just in time.

The *Hastati* surged into motion, scattering through the lower tiers, pulling civilians down into cover as screams rippled through the plaza. Somewhere beneath the thunder of boots and the clash of armor, Jesenia felt a hard grip on her arm and stumbled backward—straight into Val-Theris.

His wings folded half around her instinctively, a shield of feathers cutting her off from the sight of the crowd, his voice low but razor-edged near her ear.

"Stay near me."

She opened her mouth to argue, to say anything, but before

she could, another figure broke from the crowd. This one wasn't aiming for Val-Theris.

They were aiming for *her*. Jesenia barely saw the second blade before Val-Theris moved.

There was no hesitation as he stepped between her and the strike, his hand closing around the attacker's wrist with bone-cracking force.

The would-be assassin crumpled to the ground as guards closed in, dragging them backward through the scattering chaos. But Val-Theris didn't release Jesenia, his grip secure around her forearm.

"It's alright. You're safe," he said softly, almost to himself, though his voice trembled with a quiet fury beneath the words. "I have you."

She could hear the promise layered beneath command, and before she could respond, the plaza roared again as the crowd surged against the *Hastati*, panic threading like wildfire through their ranks.

When both attackers had been restrained, Val-Theris turned sharply, wings still half-furled around her, his gaze cutting toward the cluster of councilors at the rear steps. Varin stood at their center, calm and untouched, his expression carefully composed. But Val-Theris's stare burned like a blade driven clean through steel.

Jesenia's pulse thudded violently beneath her ribs, the truth settling cold and heavy in her chest.

Of course they had something to do with it, even if there was no proof. The attempt had been staged, engineered to rattle his authority.

It had been a message.

Val-Theris stood inches from her, his chest rising and falling in sharp, ragged breaths and his pale hair disheveled. He pulled her to the side, away from the prying eyes of the council and shielded them both with the vastness of his wings.

"You should not have done that," he said, his voice low, raw, the words more plea than scold. "If he had hurt you—"

"But he didn't," Jesenia interrupted, her voice trembling but firm. "Val-Theris, he was aiming for *you*."

His wings twitched behind him, feathers unsettled, his pale gaze fixed on her with a kind of unblinking intensity.

"You cannot–" he cut himself off, almost raggedly, *"throw yourself* between me and blades meant for my throat. I can bear my death. But I cannot—" His voice cracked with words he wouldn't dare say out loud.

I cannot bear yours.

Jesenia's heart thudded hard, her hand lifting without thought, brushing his jaw where it tightened. His skin was warm beneath her touch, trembling faintly.

"Do you understand what that would have done to me?" he asked softly. Jesenia opened her mouth, but Val-Theris cut across her silence, his voice low, ragged in a way she had never heard from him before: "I have tried to be your sovereign and friend. I have tried to be anything but this. But when that second knife struck—"

He stopped, the tension sharp in the air between them, his jaw tight, his wings trembling faintly where sunlight burned at their tips. Val-Theris reached for her, slowly, carefully, his hand trembling faintly as he lifted it toward her cheek. Jesenia didn't move, didn't breathe, letting the closeness fill the space between them like a held breath.

His fingertips brushed the curve of her jaw, like he was memorizing the shape of her. For a long, taut moment, they stared at one another, breath mingling, close enough that she could see the flecks of fury and firelight caught in his pale blue irises.

He leaned in, his forehead nearly touching hers, his hand lifting to cradle the back of her neck. The weight of the world narrowed into the heat of his breath against her lips.

Her lips parted, her breath catching. "It's okay. I'm here."

For a heartbeat, it seemed he would close the distance. His mouth hovered a whisper from hers, his hand tightening against her neck, his wings drawing in closer as though to seal them away from the world.

But then he pulled back just enough to look at her. His voice shook, but the words were steady. "Val-Oros was wrong. You will not be this kingdom's undoing."

Jesenia's body relaxed, but stiffened once more when he said:

"But I think you will be mine."

She looked up at him, her cheeks heating with something… vulnerable. "Val-Theris, don't say such things."

"I know," he said, ragged, "They would never forgive us."

They stood there, trembling, on the edge of surrender. But when footsteps echoed behind them, the spell shattered, and Val-Theris tore himself back a step, wings snapping wide in instinctive defense of their dangerous secret.

"You'll stay in the palace tonight," he said over his shoulder, his voice steady now, composed only by force of will. "I won't risk you in the streets."

Jesenia hesitated, her breath unsteady, then nodded once, holding the words she couldn't say behind her teeth. Rohannes came to her side, leading her away from the chaos and into the serenity of the gilded halls Val-Theris called home.

THE PALACE WAS silent after the chaos, but Jesenia could not rest.

She sat by the tall window in her guest chambers, the city stretching dark and restless below, her shawl wrapped tightly around her shoulders though the air was warm. Outside, Solmiris still murmured faintly with the distant crack of voices.

The door opened without warning.

Val-Theris stepped inside, the torchlight catching in the sweep of his wings, shadows pooling at his back. He wasn't armored now, only a deep crimson tunic, his expression stripped of the polished composure he wore before others.

Jesenia rose instinctively. "Val-Theris—"

He moved toward her slowly, as though unwilling to crowd her but unable to keep his distance. Her chest ached at his closeness, which suddenly felt more urgent than before. His gaze caught hers, pale and luminous, something raw burning there she'd never seen before.

His hand lifted slowly, hesitating halfway, as though asking permission without words. Jesenia didn't step back. She couldn't.

When his fingertips brushed her cheek, she felt the unmistakable tremor in him, and in that tremor was everything he wouldn't say: fear and longing and defiance sat heavy on his shoulders, threatening to break him at any moment.

"I thought I could fight this," he whispered, his voice rough against the quiet. "That I could bury it beneath duty, beneath the weight of what's expected of me. But when I saw that blade aimed at you—" His thumb brushed along her jaw, slow, deliberate, grounding himself in the warmth of her skin. "I realized I don't want to fight it anymore."

Jesenia's hand rose slowly, almost without thought, until her fingertips touched the edge of his jaw, warm and steady beneath her palm.

Neither of them moved beyond that for a moment, until Val-Theris finally pulled back just enough to look at her fully, his thumb lingering softly beneath her chin. There was no restraint left in his gaze now.

"It's not safe," Jesenia whispered finally, her voice shaking. "They tried to kill you because you gave me a voice. What will they do if you choose me?"

"I already have," Val-Theris murmured, his voice low and certain, his wings shifting faintly in the torchlight. "Every time I breathe, with whatever time I have left, Jesenia, I choose you."

And though she didn't understand why the words sounded like goodbye, they sank deep into her chest, searing and undeniable.

SIXTEEN

THE COUNCIL'S voices carried faintly down the marble corridors, muted and sharp, but Jesenia kept walking without joining them, her soft sandals whispering across the polished stone as she slipped through the quieter halls of the palace.

She needed air. Distance. Silence.

Ever since the attack in the plaza, Val-Theris had been... different.

He sought her out more often, though he rarely said why. Sometimes he'd ask her to walk the quarter with him, sometimes to sit with him in the small private library above the grand halls. Today, though, she'd chosen to avoid him, needing space to gather her thoughts before stepping into another room where his gaze would find her and undo her without meaning to.

But when she turned the corner into the high atrium, he was already there.

Val-Theris stood by the tall arched windows, the late sun setting behind him, throwing pale gold across the edges of his wings and the marble floor beneath his boots. He wasn't armored, wasn't draped in ceremony—only a simple crimson tunic, loose at the throat, and his hair unbound, falling across his brow in soft waves.

He looked like something mortal and infinite all at once.

"Val-Theris," Jesenia said softly, startled, stopping halfway across the room.

He turned his head slightly, his gaze finding hers with the quiet inevitability of a tide drawn to shore. "Once more, you weren't at the session today," he said, his voice calm but carrying something softer beneath the surface.

"I..." She hesitated, drawing her shawl closer around her shoulders. His eyes caught on the wrapping around her hand. "I thought it better to let things settle first."

"You thought it better to stay away from me," Val-Theris said.

Jesenia stilled. "I didn't say that."

"You didn't have to."

The silence stretched, taut and unyielding, filling the wide atrium like a storm. She wanted to speak, to tell him the distance was for his sake, for her people's safety, for her own sanity—but the words wouldn't form beneath the weight of his gaze, caught in the dry cowardice of her feelings.

He took a step closer, and then another, until the warm glow of sunset caught in his shimmering feathers.

Val-Theris spoke softly, his voice low and roughened at the edges, "I haven't stopped thinking about how close I came to losing you."

Jesenia tried to steady herself beneath the gravity of his words, but the space between them had grown too narrow, her pulse too loud beneath her ribs. "Val-Theris, it was hardly a close call. I think you are letting this get to you." She paused for a moment, and then looked up at him with an ache in her chest. "You should let me go," she said softly, almost pleading. "You should let me fade back into the shadows. It's safer there."

"No."

His voice was quiet, but there was steel in it, something unmovable, absolute.

He stopped close enough now that she could feel the faint heat radiating from him, close enough that the soft arch of his wing brushed against her shawl as though drawn in by her elegant gravity.

"I've been fighting this," Val-Theris said, the confession breaking from him in a voice quieter than breath. "Every day. Every time you look at me. Every time I hear your name on someone else's tongue."

Her hands trembled faintly where they clutched the folds of fabric draped across her shoulders, her heart stuttering against her ribs. She breathed his name, unsure and aching.

His hand rose slowly, hesitating just before it reached her face, his fingertips hovering like a promise he'd sworn to himself never to make.

"I can't fight it anymore," he whispered.

Jesenia's breath caught, the air between them collapsing into something smaller, denser, electric.

And then his hand touched her cheek.

It was soft, the barest graze of fingertips along her skin, but it sent her pulse surging, the world narrowing until there was nothing left but the sound of his breath and the weight of his gaze. Then Val Theris lowered his forehead until it brushed hers, his thumb stroking faintly along her jaw, the heat of him grounding her while something in his chest trembled.

"Jesenia," he said softly, her name breaking against his lips like prayer.

She answered without words, her hand rising to his wrist, her fingertips pressing lightly against his pulse where it thundered beneath her skin.

The kiss...simply happened. The tension broke, and everything that had been building, pulling them together, finally collided.

His lips brushed hers, soft and unsteady, almost as though he feared the world might shatter if he pressed harder.

It was quiet and fragile. And in that fragile infinity, Val-Theris saw it all fall apart.

The touch of her lips sent light flooding into his mind—but it wasn't solace. Flashes of imagery struck sharp and brutal.

His own blood staining broken stone. Smoke rolling through Solmiris's streets. Jesenia on her knees, her hands red where they clutched his feathers, her mouth shaping his name. A blade plunging deep beneath ribs, light scattering through his wings like glass shattering in sunlight.

And then there was silence. But it wasn't the silence of death; not that cold certainty of the end. It was worse than that, but he could not put a name to the dreadful feeling—at least not yet.

He broke the kiss sharply, his breath ragged, his hand tightening faintly against her jaw before he forced himself to let go. He touched his face and felt the smear of blood from his nose paint his fingers.

Jesenia stepped back a half-pace, her brows furrowing and her voice uneven. When she saw the blood, she reached out for him again. "Val-Theris?"

His chest heaved once, twice, his wings trembling faintly behind him as though from strain, but when he looked at her again, his expression had softened into something unbearably tender.

"I'm sorry," he whispered, though his voice carried the weight of too many meanings. "I just…couldn't wait anymore."

"You're bleeding," she said softly, brushing away the blood with her own fingers.

And though he didn't say it, though she didn't know it, the

truth burned behind his ribs like fire. He wasn't afraid of loving her anymore. He was afraid of *running out of time.*

THE WORLD CHANGED after their kiss.

Not visibly. Not to anyone else. But Jesenia felt it in the spaces where silence hung heavier than before, where the air between her and Val-Theris seemed to hum with something alive.

He had not spoken of it. Neither had she. But he came to her more often now, seeking her presence without explanation, as though drawn by something he couldn't name.

Three days had passed since the attempt in the plaza when he found her in the gardens just before dusk, perched on the low stone wall beside a bed of white blossoms. The wind tangled faint threads of her shawl as she glanced up, startled, when he stepped into view.

"Val-Theris," Jesenia said softly, rising automatically, smoothing the folds of her skirts.

"You don't have to stand," he murmured, his voice quiet, the late light catching faint gold along the edges of his feathers. "Stay."

She hesitated but sat again, her fingers brushing petals from her lap. "I thought you'd be with the council," she said after a pause, keeping her gaze on the darkening sky.

"I was," Val-Theris said simply. "I left."

Her brows knit faintly as she looked up at him. "You left a council meeting?"

"I had no interest in listening to what they had to say."

It was the truth. They had said her name too many times, and he grew tired of the bickering. Everything now was a race against time he wasn't sure he had to spare, and those moments in the chamber seemed so insignificant now.

Jesenia glanced at him sharply, but his expression was unreadable. "You've…changed," Jesenia whispered finally, hesitant but steady. "Since the attack."

Since the kiss, she wanted to add, but didn't have the strength to. His lips parted slightly, but he said nothing, his silence speaking louder than denial could.

"It feels like you're trying to be…closer," she said, her voice catching faintly on the word, "but somehow you only seem farther away."

Val-Theris's gaze softened then, his jaw shifting slightly as he lowered himself onto the stone wall beside her.

"I see things differently now. The time I have. The choices I make and the consequences that follow."

Jesenia turned toward him slightly, her brows knitting faintly. "I don't understand."

"I know," Val-Theris whispered, his gaze fixed on the slow darkening horizon. "And you don't have to. Just…stay."

For a long moment, they sat in silence, and then Val-Theris reached out, slow and deliberate, letting his hand rest atop hers where it lay in the folds of her skirt. Jesenia stilled, her breath catching sharply at the warmth of his touch, her pulse tripping unevenly beneath her ribs.

"You're holding something back," she said finally, her voice low but steady, turning her hand slightly beneath his until their fingers touched along the edges.

"Yes," he admitted softly. "But not this. I don't want to hide this."

His thumb brushed faintly along the inside of her wrist, his touch feather-light, reverent. When Jesenia glanced up, she found his gaze fixed on her. Steady, burning. Unguarded in a way she'd never seen before. Her lips parted, but before she could speak, a sharp rustle of movement drew her gaze—a servant passing the archway, pausing just a breath too long, their expression unreadable before hurrying away.

Val-Theris's hand slipped from hers slowly, his composure sliding back into place like an assassin's blade sheathed in silence.

Jesenia's heart ached with confusion and rejection. Just moments before, he claimed he did not want to hide, but closed off the moment someone saw him with her.

His hand lingered close to hers on the stone, so near their shadows almost touched in the fading sun. They both knew what it meant for them to care for each other. The council would grow bolder. The citizens more divided. The knives would sharpen, waiting for the first slip, the first weakness.

Neither of them were strong enough to let go, nor were they brave enough to face it without the other.

And Jesenia did not know the truth of what haunted him. She didn't know that every time Val-Theris looked at her now, he wasn't seeing possibility.

Only their tragedy.

Val-Theris left in silence, only pressing their foreheads together once before standing and walking away. When he was gone, the quiet of the courtyard pressed into her like a weight on her chest she was unable to lift.

She continued to sit at the edge of the fountain well into the night, her shawl pulled loosely around her shoulders, staring at the mirrored surface of the water.

"Your voice carries further than you think."

Jesenia startled slightly, turning to see Rohannes leaning against a carved stone column nearby, his helm tucked beneath one arm, his crimson-plumed crest billowing slightly in the breeze.

"I didn't hear you approach," she said softly, gathering her composure.

"You weren't meant to," he replied, crossing the courtyard until he stood opposite her, his moonlit shadow falling across the tiles. His armor caught faint glints of gold where the light broke between the trees, but his expression was unreadable.

"You've unsettled the council," Rohannes said simply.

Jesenia smoothed her shawl, her gaze falling to the slow curl of water against stone. "They resent me for speaking," she said. "And my people will resent me if nothing comes of it. Either way, I lose."

Rohannes tilted his head slightly, studying her. "And yet you speak anyway."

Jesenia met his eyes steadily, refusing to shrink beneath the gaze of him. "I cannot be silent while my people starve."

For a moment, neither of them spoke, the sound of trickling water filling the space between them. Then Rohannes stepped closer, resting his helm lightly on the low stone ledge of the fountain.

"Do you believe he favors your people above Solmiris?" he asked, voice low, even.

Jesenia hesitated, fingers curling faintly into her shawl. "I don't know what I believe," she admitted. "I think he wants my people to thrive here, but won't use his authority to make it so. I think he sees too much, tries to carry too much. No matter what he decides, someone suffers for it. He is consumed by trying to determine whose suffering is easier to swallow than the other."

Rohannes studied her for a long moment, his dark green eyes narrowing faintly as if weighing his words. When he finally spoke, his voice was quieter than before, lower, almost conspiratorial.

"You should trust him."

Jesenia blinked, surprised by the firmness of it. "Trust him?"

"Yes," Rohannes said softly. "Even when you don't understand him. Especially then."

Her brows drew together faintly. "You speak as if you know something I don't."

"I know my king," he replied simply, leaning one hand against the fountain's edge, his armor whispering faintly as he shifted closer. "I was a soldier of Korvath, you know. I defected and came to him, ashamed of what I had done in his brother's name. He never held it against me, and I've earned my place at his side. I've stood by him through many things and watched helplessly as that crown weighed him down. I know this with certainty, Jesenia: every choice he makes costs him something. Sometimes everything."

She looked at him, quiet, searching his face for something he wasn't saying.

And then, softly, she asked, "How can I trust him when I don't know his heart?"

Rohannes held her gaze for a long moment, the silence stretching thin between them before he finally spoke, his words careful:

"You should not mistake his silence for indifference. You are not wrong to care for your people, but Val-Theris carries burdens you cannot see."

Jesenia stilled, her breath catching faintly at the weight in his tone. "You speak of his foresight."

Before she could press further, Rohannes pushed off from the fountain's edge, sliding his helm back beneath his arm. He paused at the threshold, his back half-turned, his voice carrying softer now, almost as if to himself.

"Sometimes, Lady Jesenia, the path ahead isn't chosen. It's endured."

SEVENTEEN

The council chamber was already loud when Jesenia entered. It wasn't filled with shouting, but with the low, grinding noise of men who believed they knew all—men who believed their cruelty justified. Voices overlapped in measured indignation, robes rustled, rings tapped impatiently against marble. The long table gleamed beneath the afternoon light, gold inlay catching against the polished stone, beautiful in a way that felt obscene when weighed against the hunger she had just walked through to get here.

Val-Theris stood at the head of the chamber, wings folded tight behind him, expression carefully neutral. He did not look at her when she entered, though she felt the subtle shift in his posture—the acknowledgment that she was there.

She took her place at the table to his right, hands folded, shawl drawn close.

"The unrest in the lower districts is no longer contained," Councilor Varin said, his voice smooth with displeasure. "The ration lines were disrupted this morning. A guard injured. Another nearly stabbed. The people grow bold."

"That is a lie!" Jesenia said before she could stop herself. "My people have never hurt any of your citizens. It is *your* people who incite the unrest."

The room went still. Jesenia had never spoken so boldly before, but she was irritated with the council and pacifism did not mean she had endless patience.

Varin's mouth curled faintly. "Ah. The Lunarethian speaks."

Jesenia straightened. "My people stood in line as they always do. Some of them were turned away after hours of waiting. Mothers with children. Elderly men who can no longer stand for long periods. If desperation looks like boldness to you, perhaps you have forgotten what hunger does to the body."

A murmur rippled through the chamber. Another councilor leaned forward, palms pressed flat against the table. "We cannot continue diverting supplies to the quarter at the expense of our own citizens."

"They are under your protection now. Does that mean nothing?"

"It means they are guests," Varin snapped. "And guests do not dictate the household."

Val-Theris lifted a hand. "Enough." The room quieted, but the tension did not lift. "We are here to discuss solutions," he said evenly. "Not to assign blame."

"With respect, Majesty," another councilor interjected, "the solution is obvious. We limit rations further until order is restored."

The words hit Jesenia like a physical blow. She stood, heart hammering. "You would starve them into silence?"

Several heads turned. One man laughed softly, without humor. "They are already starving," he said. "We would simply... hasten compliance."

Val-Theris's wings twitched. "That will not happen," he said, voice quiet and firm.

Varin raised a brow. "Then perhaps Your Majesty would like to explain how we are to feed these guests without stealing from Seraveth's mouths?"

"There are surplus stores in the eastern granaries," Jesenia said quickly. "You know this. I've seen the ledgers. There are less than ninety Lunarethians within your walls. I am not asking you to feed an army, I am begging you to show some humanity to people who have lost everything."

"You have seen no such thing," Varin cut in sharply. "You are not a councilor. You do not have the authority to view those records."

"She reviewed the documents with my permission," Val-Theris said.

The room stiffened.

"And therein lies the problem," Varin replied calmly. "You give her leave. You walk among her people. You listen to her counsel. The city sees this, Majesty. They whisper. They ask why a foreign woman is granted the ear of a god while citizens born beneath your banners go unheard."

Jesenia felt her chest tighten. "You think this is about *me*," she said, incredulous. "While children are starving in your streets?"

"It is about perception," Varin said coolly. "And perception governs loyalty."

Val-Theris said nothing. Jesenia turned to him, disbelief creeping into her voice, then looked back to Varin. "You can open the granaries today. Even temporarily. Even just until winter—"

"And what happens after winter thaws?" another councilor demanded. "And the day after? When the people realize all they must do to bend the crown is riot loudly enough?"

"They're not rioting," Jesenia said. "They're begging."

"Begging is simply a kinder word for demanding," Varin replied. "And demand becomes revolt."

"And starving becomes death," she shot back, her composure finally cracking. "Is that an acceptable cost to you? Are you really so afraid of pacifists who let Korvath destroy their homes because they would not fight back?"

The chamber erupted. Voices rose, overlapping, sharp with accusation and fear.

"Your voice is the reason the Lunarethians are so comfortable inciting unrest. You have no understanding of governance! This is exactly why it was a mistake allowing you to enter this chamber."

Val-Theris stood motionless amid it all. Jesenia waited. She waited for him to raise his voice. To strike the table. To remind them who he was. But he didn't.

Instead, he lifted a single hand. The room fell silent again.

"We will revisit ration distribution at the next session," he said. "For now, this discussion is concluded."

Jesenia stared at him. That was it. No concessions. No immediate relief. Just postponement that might as well have been a slap in the face.

She looked toward him, unable to keep the tremor from her voice. "Val-Theris—"

"Not now," he said quietly.

Something inside her snapped. She turned away from the council, away from their polished indifference, and walked straight toward the doors.

Behind her, Varin exhaled in thin satisfaction, and rose from his seat with a triumphant smile that faded the moment his king stood to follow the refugee through the door.

THE DOOR to Val-Theris's private office slammed shut behind Jesenia, and the sound echoed through the marble chamber like a crack of thunder.

Val-Theris had followed her inside, then stood at the window, his wings drawn tight against his back, their golden edges dim in the afternoon light.

"You can't keep turning them away," Jesenia said, her voice trembling with fury and grief. "There are children starving in the refugee quarter, Val-Theris. The ration lines barely last an hour before the guards shut them down. The council keeps promising more supplies but nothing ever comes!"

"I know," he said quietly.

"Then do something!"

He turned, eyes hardening. "It's not that simple."

"It *is* that simple!" she snapped, stepping closer. "You are the King of Seraveth! You are a god among men! You could open the granaries today if you wanted to!"

He looked away. "And if I do, I give the council cause to call me a tyrant."

"Better a tyrant who feeds the hungry than a king who watches them die!"

Her words hit him like a slap. For a moment, he said nothing, only let the silence stretch until it was unbearable.

"You think I don't want to help them?" His voice was low now, controlled, but shaking beneath the surface. "You think I don't hear their cries in my sleep? Every petition I grant, every law I sign—it's a war with my own council. They control the trade routes. They own the fields. I may be a god, but the crown is not, Jesenia. It is a cage."

"Then break it!" she cried. "You of all people can!"

Her words trembled in the air between them. He stared at her for a long time, his expression unreadable. Then, very softly, he said, "If I do what you ask...I will be no better than my brother."

Jesenia shook her head. "You are *nothing* like him."

"Am I not?" he demanded, stepping forward, the air shifting with the faint stir of his wings. "You think Val-Oros began his rule by burning cities? No. He began by believing his godhood gave him the right to ignore law. By believing that his heart was wiser than the balance of his people. I will *not* become that."

Her voice cracked. "Then what good is your mercy if it starves us?"

Val-Theris went still. For the first time, she saw something almost fragile in his face—that flicker of doubt he could never admit. But it hardened again, quickly, as though he feared what it might mean to let her see it.

"You speak like someone who's never ruled," he said finally, his tone cutting. "You don't understand what's at stake."

"I understand hunger," she shot back. "I understand watching people die because no one in power cares enough to stop it!"

He raised his voice. Something he'd never done to her before. "You're being unreasonable."

Her breath caught. "*Unreasonable?*"

"Yes," he said, the word sharp as glass. "You're letting your heart blind you to what must be done. This is not the time to let your emotions get in the way."

The air left the room. Jesenia's lips parted, but no sound came. He knew, instantly, what he'd said—that it was the same words the council had used against her, the same insult that stripped her of her voice in that chamber time and time again.

Emotional. Unreasonable. Ignorant.

She blinked rapidly, tears stinging her eyes. "I see," she whispered.

"Jesenia—"

"No." She shook her head, stepping back. "You've made yourself clear." She turned and walked toward the door, her steps soft against the marble.

"Jesenia, please—"

But she was gone. The door closed quietly behind her, but to Val-Theris, it might as well have been the sound of a blade sinking into his chest. He stood there for a long time, hands trembling at his sides, staring at the door she'd just walked through.

What have I done? he thought to himself. The silence stretched until a voice broke it.

"She's right, you know."

Val-Theris turned sharply. Rohannes stood by one of the pillars near the door, his expression unreadable. "You heard," the king said.

"I hear everything," Rohannes replied. "As is my job."

Val-Theris exhaled, pressing his hand to his temple. "Was I too harsh?"

Rohannes hesitated before answering. "No. You were honest. And you were not wrong—feeding the Lunarethians without the council's consent would start a civil war."

Val-Theris looked at him, eyes hollow. "And yet?"

"And yet," Rohannes said quietly, "she wasn't wrong either."

Val-Theris turned away, his shoulders heavy. "Do you ever tire of reminding me that I am both a savior and an executioner?"

Rohannes smiled faintly. "Every day, Majesty."

He stepped forward, laying a steady hand on his King's arm. "She'll forgive you. She always does."

Val-Theris didn't answer, for he wasn't sure he believed it.

Meanwhile, the corridors of the palace stretched endlessly ahead of Jesenia. The gilded marble and soft torchlight that held a beauty which mocked the emptiness and helplessness inside her.

She didn't remember how she'd gotten here. Only that one moment she'd been standing before Val-Theris, her heart breaking with every word, and the next, she was walking away because staying had hurt too much.

Her footsteps echoed softly. She passed the carved archways, the murals of angels and kings, the gold-leafed symbols of divine grace. They seemed hollow now, like paintings made for people blind to the reality of the world they live in.

When she reached her chambers, she shut the door behind her and leaned against it, closing her eyes. For a long while, she didn't move. The silence pressed against her ears until she could hear her own heartbeat, uneven and fast.

Outside, Solmiris glittered under the night sky, a city of light and gold.

But from where she stood, it was only a false reflection; the glow of lanterns hiding the hunger in the streets below.

AFTER VAL-THERIS FINISHED his work with the council, he found Jesenia's chambers without thought, his boots soundless on polished marble. He did not knock, he simply entered her room and closed the door softly behind him.

She sat by the window, her knees drawn up, her bare feet tucked beneath her skirts, the late sun spilling sharp across her bruised cheek.

When Val-Theris stepped inside, she didn't turn.

"You shouldn't be here," Jesenia said quietly, her voice steady but hollow.

He froze, his jaw tightening faintly. "I needed to see you. To apologize for what I said earlier."

Her laugh was soft, bitter, and without warmth. "This is much bigger than you or I. You know this."

"Yes I do," he agreed, chest constricting. He forced himself forward, closer to her. "But what I've come for is about…us. Not politics."

"Is it?" Jesenia finally turned to face him, her dark eyes flashing beneath the bruises and ash. "The entire city whispers about me. *The foreign girl. The king's whore.* You put me there, Val-Theris—you made me this. All of this is because I asked for a warm meal."

Her voice broke faintly, the words trembling in the stillness.

"I will not hear that from you."

Jesenia lowered her gaze, fingers curling into the edge of her shawl. "Since the day we met, everything has been worse," she whispered. "Your people hate mine. The council schemes behind your back to overthrow everything you've built. And my people —" Her voice caught faintly, thin with exhaustion. "They now look at me as though I've traded their safety for my seat at your table. And today," Jesenia whispered, trembling despite herself, "it was just a reminder that nothing I do can change that."

The sound of her voice breaking where she rarely allowed it to sliced deeper than any blade. He crossed the remaining distance between them slowly, cautiously, until the sun caught the faint tremor in his feathers.

"I swore I would help you and your people," he whispered, his voice barely audible, "and every time I fail, they find new ways to make you bleed for it."

"Then stop," Jesenia snapped, her voice louder now, the emotion breaking through exhaustion. "Stop choosing me, Val-Theris! Stop giving them reasons to punish my people for my existence!"

Her words echoed between them, the silence afterward heavy and sharp. But Val-Theris didn't flinch. Instead, his voice came quiet, steady, and full of something deeper than command.

"I can't."

Jesenia shook her head sharply, frustrated tears stinging the edges of her vision. "Why?" she demanded, her voice shaking now as she stood to face him fully. "Why can't you just let me go back to being a foreign girl in the shadows?"

"Because I don't have time to."

The words stilled her. Val-Theris exhaled slowly, his wings trembling faintly before folding tighter against his back, his gaze locked unblinking on hers. His jaw tightened faintly, his breath uneven as his hand lifted, stopping just shy of her bruised cheek—hovering there, close enough to feel the warmth of her skin.

"I've seen my death."

Jesenia blinked, the silence ringing sharp between them. "What?"

"The day I kissed you," Val-Theris murmured, his voice distant, reverent and haunted all at once. "I saw it—the blade that ends me. And you were there, grieving for me. That's why I can't let you go," Val-Theris said, his voice raw now, threaded through with something soft and devastating. "I will die, Jesenia. Soon. And until that day comes, I am going to choose you over my council."

Tears blurred her vision before she realized they were falling. She wanted to scream at him, to tell him she hated him for tethering her to his death, to his fate—and yet beneath the anger, fear churned deeper than anything she could voice.

She pressed a hand over her mouth, steadying her breath as she stepped back from him, shaking her head. "You should have told me," she whispered, her voice breaking on the edges of the words. "You should have let me decide if I wanted this knowing what comes."

Val-Theris closed the distance between them slowly, his hand finally brushing along her cheek, his thumb warm and reverent where it caught the edge of her tears.

"Would you choose any differently?" he asked softly.

"No," she admitted.

For a moment, silence stretched, the weight of everything unsaid pressing sharp between them. Val-Theris's forehead lowered, almost brushing hers, his breath unsteady, his wings half-spread behind him as if instinct sought to shelter her even now.

Jesenia's throat tightened, her breath uneven as she finally met his gaze. For a long moment, she said nothing. And then, very softly, she asked:

"What would it take to stop this hatred between my people and yours? Is there really nothing you can do, Val-Theris? As king?"

Val-Theris stilled, his wings tightening faintly behind him. The silence between them stretched taut, filled only by the racing thoughts in his mind. For a long moment, neither spoke. Then Val-Theris drew a quiet, steadying breath.

"Marry me."

Jesenia froze, the words hanging in the air like struck glass. "What?"

"I'll make it official," Val-Theris said, his voice calm but threaded with an urgency he couldn't disguise; an urgency to fix what neither of them could see was broken beyond repair. "If you become my queen, your people will be granted full citizenship—protections, provisions, freedom to move and trade without restriction. No more camps. No more slurs spat in the streets. No more riots."

She stared at him, the sunlight painting sharp edges across his face, her pulse loud in her ears.

"You want to marry me for politics," she clarified, hurt on her tongue.

"No," he said quickly, leaning forward slightly, his gaze locked on hers. "I want to marry you because I care about you and don't want to see any more suffering in my walls. It will give me the power to protect you and your people."

Jesenia's breath caught, but instead of relief, something sharp cracked in her chest.

"Do you?" she whispered, barely audible.

Val-Theris stilled. "Do I what?"

"Do you care about me?" she said, louder this time, her voice shaking. "Or do you just value the ease I bring to your conscience?" She stood slowly, clutching her shawl more securely around her, stepping back from him as the words spilled. "I was foolish," she whispered. "I thought you…I thought *we* were real, Val-Theris. That what we had could have been more someday. But now…" Her voice faltered as she shook her head, staring down at her scraped palms. "Now I wonder if you only ever wanted me because I was useful."

"That's not true," Val-Theris said sharply, rising to follow her, his wings flaring faintly behind him as if they reflected the strain in his voice. "Jesenia, I would bleed for you—"

"You would turn my name into a shield," she cut back, her voice trembling. "A weapon I never wanted to be. Something to wield when the council corners you. An excuse to undermine them. And I would spend the rest of my life wondering if I was your wife or your banner of triumph."

The silence that followed struck harder than the shouting in the streets.

"I want to marry for love," she whispered, her voice breaking softly around the edges. "Not to fix your ongoing war with your own people."

Val-Theris's throat worked, but no words came. He looked at her as if reaching for something already lost, his breath uneven as his wings slowly folded close behind him.

"Jesenia," he tried softly, but she shook her head once, stepping away.

"No," she said, her voice trembling but firm. "Not like this."

She left him standing in her room as the sun climbed higher, his shadow stretched long across the pale marble floors. The seconds ticked away, the vision of his own death burning beneath his ribs, knowing time was a luxury he could not afford to lose, and somehow lost it anyway.

From that day forward, something in the city shifted. Anytime Val-Theris came searching, Jesenia always found some reason to disappear before he arrived. She was avoiding him, and that hollowed him out in ways he never expected.

The council noticed her absence in the halls of the palace, and Varin was the first to use it like a poison. Softly. Skillfully. Like slipping a few drops into his wine just to see how much it would take to kill a god.

At first, Val-Theris ignored his remarks. But the whispers grew louder, spreading beyond the marble halls and into the streets until even soldiers murmured questions in the guard-rooms, until traders passed gossip across stalls as if trading currency.

And Jesenia, hearing the same words echoed in shadows, pulled further away.

He tried to reach her.

He tried until exhaustion carved hollows beneath his eyes, until the parchment stacks on his desk blurred beneath sleepless nights. He tried to speak to her. To explain. To hold her without words and let her feel what he couldn't seem to say out loud.

To let her hear the words that were too dangerous to leave his throat.

THE HIGH COUNCIL chamber glimmered with cold light, the dawn spilling warm gold through its high arched windows. Val-Theris stood at the head of the marble table, his wings folded tight against his back, the weight of a dozen eyes fixed on him. They had called him for an emergency session which he had denied—thrice—before answering the summons.

Councilor Gena's voice was the first to break the silence. "You shame us, Your Majesty."

The words echoed sharply across the marble floor. Val-Theris's jaw tightened, but he said nothing as Gena leaned forward, her thin fingers tapping against the table.

"You bring that Lunarethian girl into our sacred halls, and now the entire city whispers of it. Do you think your people kneel to you because of sentiment?" Her smile was faint, cold. "No. They kneel because they believe you are more than a man. And yet for nearly a week's time, you mope about like a heart-broken boy."

A low murmur of agreement rippled through the chamber.

Councilor Varin struck next, his voice heavy. "We tolerated the refugee's presence because she kept her head bowed. But now you flaunt her, let her into your chambers overnight, sulk when she denies you, and *worse*—rumor says you've laid with her! Tell me, your Majesty, are you Solmiris's king or a reckless child playing house?"

Something in him snapped.

Val-Theris's wings unfurled wide with a sound like thunder, their span filling the chamber, feathers scattering faint motes of dust from the air. His eyes, usually soft and unreadable, burned fierce as steel struck with flame.

I am your king, he said, his voice low, carrying like a blade through silence. "Do not mistake my patience for weakness." The councilors stilled, but he did not stop. He stepped forward, his boots striking the polished marble, his gaze cutting across them like fire. "You sit in these gilded chairs and scold me as though I am your son. But it is I who bleeds for this throne. It is I who sees futures none of you dare imagine. And it is I who carries Seraveth upon his shoulders while you trade whispers and count coins."

His hand slammed flat against the marble table, the crack echoing through the dome. "You call Lady Jesenia a weakness. I tell you this: she holds more strength than all of us combined. You will not speak of her as filth beneath your shoes again."

The silence that followed was suffocating. Gena's lips pressed thin, her knuckles against the table edge. "This city bows to a god, not a man who gives his heart to foreign blood. If you insist on dragging us into ruin, we will—"

"You will what?" Val-Theris cut her off, his voice low, dangerous. His wings spread wider still, the sunlight catching their edges until they glowed faintly. "Depose me? You forget yourselves. Without me, Seraveth is nothing but marble and dust. Remember that before you ever dare raise your tongue to me again."

No one spoke after that.

One by one, the councilors rose, their expressions tight with fury and fear. They bowed stiffly with the hollow submission of those already planning treachery, and filed out of the chamber. When the doors shut, Val-Theris stood alone, his chest heaving faintly, his hands braced hard against the marble table.

The council would never forgive him for allying himself with Jesenia.

And she would never forgive him for making her a symbol of mercy in a kingdom too proud to accept it.

EIGHTEEN

VAL-THERIS LEFT them behind with their pale faces and stiff bows, with their half-swallowed threats and careful hatred, and the silence that followed him down the corridors felt louder than any shout.

He walked without destination at first.

His boots made no sound on the marble, but he could feel the echo of each step through his bones. The murals of angels watched him pass—painted eyes forever benevolent, forever serene.

His wings were still half-fanned with the aftershock of rage, feathers unsettled. It was not the kind of anger he indulged often. It left him hollow afterward, as if each outburst tore away something he needed to keep himself intact.

By the time he reached the upper residence wing, the sun had lowered into late afternoon. The light slanted through high arched windows in sharp bars, gilding the dust in the air and turning it into something almost holy. The palace smelled faintly of incense and old parchment and polished stone.

None of it soothed him.

He stopped outside Jesenia's chambers.

For a long moment, he stood there with his hand hovering over the door as if he could feel her on the other side. He had not seen her since the day she left him standing in her room with the sunlight cutting him into pieces. Since the day his noble intention had turned into a weapon in her hands because it had not been offered as a choice, but as a solution.

He had tried to tell himself that time would soften it. He had tried to believe Rohannes when he said she always forgave.

But the memory of her face when she asked—*Do you care about me, or do you just value the ease I bring to your conscience?*—had not left him. It haunted him more deeply than visions ever had, because it was real and present and he could not outrun it.

He knocked. Once. Twice.

No answer.

He could have left. He should have left. He had no right to enter uninvited after everything he'd done.

But his patience—his careful restraint—had already been spent in the council chamber. And the thought of her sitting alone with that same bitterness twisting in her chest while the city sharpened its knives…it was unbearable.

He opened the door.

The room was dimmer than he expected, the curtains half-drawn to keep out the glare. The late sun still found its way through, pooling in puddles of gold along the floorboards and catching on the edge of the small table near the window.

She was not there. He hadn't expected her to be, but a part of him clung to the hope of possibility. The only other place she would be in a city that hated her was down in the refugee quarter with her people, trying to soothe the suffering brought upon by his own.

He walked there alone, slowly, like he was afraid at any moment for the Lunarethians to push back on his presence. But in fact, they hardly noticed him at all, like he was simply an apparition patrolling their makeshift tents and small fires.

His eyes landed on a washbasin with Jesenia among the three women sitting around it, scrubbing dirt from linens and children's clothes. He watched her for a while, the way her brow furrowed in concentration as she used a stone to wear away at a stain. Her eyes seemed dark with sorrow and heartbreak.

Val-Theris had come to learn that she kept her hands busy when her mind was full, to try and calm her racing thoughts—but he could tell that whatever sat at the forefront of her mind would not let her forget so easily.

Her hair was loose down her back. Her shawl was wrapped tightly around her shoulders. The faint bruise along her cheekbone was yellowing at the edges now, as if time was trying to heal what the city insisted on reopening.

She didn't turn when he stepped closer. "You shouldn't be here," she said quietly without lifting her head.

Her voice was steady. Hollow. That was worse than fury. Val-Theris kneeled next to her as softly as he could, as though the slowness might reduce the damage of his presence. He did not approach like a king or a god. He approached like a man who had already broken something precious and was trying not to shatter what remained.

"I know," he said. "But please, I need to speak with you."

"I've been trying to be gone," Jesenia replied without looking at him. "That is the point. But you make it difficult when you come looking for me."

Val-Theris swallowed. "I don't want to fight with you," he said.

Jesenia finally turned her head slightly. Not fully. Just enough for him to see the edge of her expression.

"You don't want to fight," she echoed, almost amused, but the sound held no humor. "You made a proposal that would have turned my body into a treaty and my heart into collateral, and you don't want to fight."

Val-Theris did not flinch. He deserved the words. Every one of them.

"I was wrong," he said quietly. The sentence hung between them, stark and simple, without justification or excuse. Jesenia's eyes narrowed faintly, as though she didn't trust the shape of it. His wings folded tighter behind him, a habit he could not break—making himself smaller when he felt too large for the moment.

"I've spent days trying to find a way to explain myself," he said. "I've filled entire pages in my head with words that sound noble and necessary. Citizenship. Protections. Food. Safety. The end of slurs and camps and ration lines." His voice roughened. "And none of it changes what you said to me. That you wanted to marry for love, not as a political solution. And I tried to take that from you for...*convenience*."

He cringed at the harshness of the word, but somehow, it felt like the only one that fit.

Jesenia dried her hands on the fabric of her dress at her thighs before her hands tightened around the edge of her shawl. Then she stood and stepped away from the others to make the conversation more private. Val-Theris followed to the edge of an alley, where she stared at him as if he were something new—something she didn't want to let herself believe in.

Val-Theris looked down at the ground for a moment, as though he could find humility there.

"In that moment," he admitted, "I wasn't thinking of you as Jesenia."

Her breath caught faintly. He lifted his gaze again.

"I was thinking of you as a way out." The truth hurt to say. It scraped his throat raw. "A way out of the council," he continued. "A way out of their control. A way to prove to the city that the refugees were not vermin, not burdens, not—"

He stopped, jaw tightening.

"I tried to turn you into a banner," he said quietly. "I tried to hang your name over the gates and hope it would make them ashamed of their cruelty."

Jesenia's eyes glistened, but she did not blink. She held his gaze like a blade.

"And did you think it would work?" she asked.

Val-Theris exhaled slowly. "I *didn't* think," he said. "Not as I should have."

The confession was too human. Too bare. It felt like stripping armor in a room full of knives. He stepped closer again, slowly, stopping when his boots met her toes. Close enough to be heard clearly. Far enough not to trap her.

"You asked me if I cared about you," he said, voice low. "And I answered you with policy. I tried to offer you a crown you didn't want and called it freedom, when really it was just a cage that gave you a nicer title."

Jesenia's throat bobbed. Her jaw trembled once before she mastered it. That finally made her look fully at him. Her eyes were dark, rimmed with exhaustion and something sharper— something that had learned to survive by not trusting mercy, even when it came in divine hands. Val-Theris glanced toward the quarter and beyond, toward the distant glow of the city.

"I wanted to fix it," he said, and the words were almost a whisper. "I wanted one decisive action. One thing I could do that would make them stop hurting you."

Jesenia's voice thinned. "And you didn't think that you'd be hurting me?"

Val-Theris closed his eyes briefly, as if bracing himself.

"I did," he admitted. "Some part of me did." He opened his eyes again. "And I did it anyway because I thought the ends would justify it. Because I thought my intentions would make it clean. That you might see what your people needed and understand. That…you'd give them one more part of yourself when I had no right to ask that of you."

His gaze held hers. Jesenia did not speak, but the air changed. She listened. Val-Theris's wings shifted faintly, feathers brushing against one another with a soft, restless sound. "I cannot change what I said," he said softly. "I cannot undo the way it made you feel. But I can tell you what I should have told you then."

Jesenia's hands loosened slightly on her shawl. Her gaze remained guarded. Val-Theris bowed his head a fraction—an acknowledgment that felt almost ceremonial.

"I want you by my side," he said quietly. "Not as an answer. Not as a symbol. Not as a chess piece to corner my council. I want you because you are Jesenia. Because you walk through starvation and still find room to carry others. Because you have every reason to hate my city and yet you keep saving the people within it. Because your courage shames both men and gods, and I am jealous of how you do it so easily."

Jesenia's lips parted. Her breath trembled.

"I came here to say that I was wrong," he continued. "And that I am sorry for using your gentle heart to try and solve problems you never created."

Jesenia stared at him for a long time. Finally, she spoke. "You wanted to marry me," she said slowly, "so that my people could stop starving."

Val-Theris nodded once. "Yes."

"And you believed it was noble."

"Yes."

"And you didn't stop to consider that making me your queen would paint a target on my back larger than anything I've ever known."

Val-Theris's throat worked. "I did consider it," he admitted. "And I chose to ignore it, believing I could protect you from any threat that followed." Val-Theris's hand lifted as if to reach for her, then stopped, hovering in the air between them before lowering again. He did not touch without permission. "I am used to choosing," he said. "Kings choose. Gods choose. We decide and the world obeys or breaks."

His gaze held hers with painful steadiness.

"And then you looked at me and asked if what we had was real…and I realized I had been treating you like an outcome."

Jesenia's eyes shone now, tears held in place by sheer force.

"What we have *is* real," she whispered, as if the words hurt to say. "Or it *was*. Until you made me feel like…like you'd chosen me because it solved a problem."

Val-Theris took a slow breath. He stepped back half a pace— not retreating, but giving her space as if space was the only thing he could offer properly.

"I cannot promise you that I will fix Seraveth," he said. "I cannot promise you the council will ever meet me halfway. I cannot promise you the people will stop whispering." His eyes softened. "But I can promise you this: I will never again ask you to sacrifice your heart for my war."

Jesenia stared at him, and something in her expression wavered—like a wall cracking.

"You don't understand," she said quietly. "When you offered me marriage like that, it felt like you were asking me to be grateful."

Val-Theris's brow furrowed.

"Grateful to be chosen," she continued, voice trembling now. "Grateful to be pulled out of the mud and placed in your palace. As if I should thank you for giving me a place at your table while my people starve beneath your walls."

Val-Theris's face twisted with pain. "I never wanted you to feel that," he said.

"But I did," Jesenia replied, and her voice finally broke. "And for a moment, I regretted every moment we spent together—I questioned every conversation, every gaze, every touch—wondering if it was all part of some ulterior motive I was too foolish to see."

Jesenia wiped at her cheek with the edge of her shawl, but the tears kept coming, quiet and steady.

"I hate your council," she said, voice raw. "I hate the way they look at me. I hate the way your people spit my name like it's poison." Her breath hitched. "But I do not hate you."

The confession filled the space between them. Val-Theris's throat tightened. He looked down, as if the emotion might be too much to hold in her gaze.

"Jesenia," he said softly.

She shook her head once, cutting him off—not cruelly, but because she needed to say it before she lost the courage. "I don't forgive easily," she whispered. "We Lunarethians don't have the luxury of forgiving people who hurt us, because most of the time the people who hurt us don't stop."

Val-Theris held still, listening.

"But you," she continued, voice trembling with something like grief, "you did stop. You came here. You said you were wrong." She swallowed hard. "I've been waiting for someone powerful to admit that. Even once. And I don't know what to do with that," she admitted. "Because part of me wants to stay angry. Part of me wants to keep my distance so you can't hurt me like that again."

Val-Theris's voice was barely audible. "I understand."

Jesenia let out a slow, shaking breath.

"But another part of me," she said softly, "remembers the way you looked at me when I stepped through those gates and I saw you standing above the plaza. That moment when our gazes collided and it seemed like you were remembering me from a time that had not happened yet. Like I wasn't just a foreigner in your city. Like I mattered in some way."

Val-Theris's chest rose with a restrained breath.

"You do matter," he said quietly.

Jesenia nodded once, tears still slipping down her cheeks. "Then don't ask me to be your solution," she said. "Ask me to be your partner."

Val-Theris went utterly still. "If you forgive me," he said quietly, "I will spend the rest of my life proving that you were not wrong to."

Jesenia closed her eyes for a long moment. When she opened them, her gaze was still guarded. But softer.

"I forgive you," she said, but it came out like it was the hardest thing she ever had to say.

Val-Theris's breath left him like he had been holding it for days. His hand lifted again—slow, tentative. He waited, eyes searching hers for permission rather than assuming it. Jesenia did not move away. So he touched her, his fingertips along her cheek where the bruise still lingered, warm and careful as prayer.

"I'm sorry," he whispered.

Jesenia's eyes closed briefly under the touch.

"I know," she whispered back.

Val-Theris leaned forward, resting his forehead against hers. His wings shifted, folding slightly around her without fully enclosing—an instinct tempered by restraint to preserve the moment and shield them from eyes that did not deserve to see them.

He moved away slightly to meet her eyes once more, and offered her his hand.

And she took it without hesitation.

NINETEEN

From this height, Solmiris was nothing more than a shimmer of gold veins in the dark—its towers and bridges softened by the night wind, its noise swallowed by distance.

Val-Theris stood at the edge of the parapet, wings folded loosely behind him. The moonlight caught along the curve of each feather, turning him into something that could not hide its divinity. He had brought Jesenia to a place that few knew of, and none could enter without the flight he was born with.

It was a platform of marble high in the mountains, above the golden dome of the palace. It offered an unobscured view of the city below, and the world beyond stretched for miles upon miles.

Jesenia stepped closer, her breath visible in the cool air. "I didn't know there was a way up here," she said quietly.

"There isn't," he replied, looking back at her with a small, knowing smile. "Not for anyone else."

"It's breathtaking." She glanced to her feet, where a blanket covered the marble, and a pitcher of wine sat next to a basket of fruit. "Why bring me?"

"Because this is the only place in the kingdom that doesn't

belong to anyone but me," he said. "And I wanted you to share it with me—to see what it feels like to be free in my city."

They sat together on the ledge, the wind teasing her hair into soft threads of silver. Jesenia drew her knees closer, tucking her hands beneath her shawl, though she was not cold. Not next to him, at least.

"You bring me to places like this," she said at last, her voice low, careful, "and I forget that I do not belong."

Val-Theris turned his head slightly, studying her profile in the moonlight. "You do belong," he said quietly. "Damn what anyone else may have to say about it. You do belong, Jesenia. Right here. With me. And I do not want to pretend otherwise anymore."

Her breath caught, subtle but unmistakable. She looked at him then, at the calm gravity in his expression, at the restraint etched into the way he held himself, as though every instinct urged him forward and every oath held him back.

"What are you saying?" she asked.

He hesitated. That alone was answer enough. Jesenia searched his face, as if looking for command there, or expectation. She found neither. She reached out before she quite realized she was going to, her fingers brushing his wrist where his sleeve ended. The contact was light, almost tentative, but she felt the way his breath changed at once.

"I don't know what tomorrow will bring. I don't know what our people may ask of us. And I can't say what this city will do once it realizes how I truly feel for you. But I do know this." He used his thumb and forefinger to lift her chin and leaned in, so that his breath ghosted over her lips. "I will no longer pretend that what I feel is something smaller than it is for the sake of others. You deserve all of me."

Slowly, he moved his fingers from her chin to her cheek, then traced his thumb along her lower lip.

"May I?" he asked.

The question undid her more than any boldness could have. Jesenia nodded once, breath unsteady, and leaned into his touch. The space between them dissolved.

His mouth found hers—tentative at first, then deeper, desperate, as though the years he'd spent restrained had finally broken all at once. Her hands rose to his shoulders, her fingers tracing the ridges of his wings, marveling at the warmth beneath the feathers.

But it was when Jesenia's hand threaded into his hair that he lost himself in her.

The kiss deepened. His restraint shattered at the heat rising beneath their skin, hands wandering in desperation. His mouth traced the line of her jaw, her throat, while she gasped his name against his ear, her fingers clutching the fabric of his tunic as though to anchor herself.

"Tell me to stop," he whispered raggedly against her skin. "And I will."

She shook her head, her voice breaking as she pulled him closer. "Don't you dare."

And with that, the angel and the saint surrendered at last.

They sank together onto the marble, the cold stone forgotten beneath the press of bodies and breath. Above them, the stars burned like watching eyes, but for once, the heavens were kind to them where the people were not.

Time fractured into softness they had never dared share before. The sound of sighs, the brush of skin against skin, the whispered prayer of her name on his lips.

His hands studied her carefully, tracing the lines of her body with all the care and devotion as if she were born a goddess herself. He moved as if she were something holy—touched as if she was made of all the beauty this world had to give.

When it was over, they lay entwined in silence, the night

wrapping them in its vast, forgiving arms. His wing curved protectively around her, sheltering her from the wind and preserving the warmth their bodies had created together.

"What do you see when you look at the stars?" she asked drowsily.

"This," he murmured. "All of my dreams, even the ones I didn't know I had, were gifted to me under these very stars. What more beauty could I ask of them?" He looked down at her, tracing the line of her jaw with his thumb. "And what do you see when you look at these same stars?"

"A future where we don't have to hide."

He pressed a kiss to her temple. "Then this place will be our secret."

Jesenia's eyes drifted shut, her breathing slowing. Val-Theris watched her a long while, the weight of prophecy far from his mind.

"A future where I give you your dreams as you have given me mine," he murmured into her hair as he held her. "That is what I see when I look at the stars now."

TWENTY

Rohannes intercepted the courier before he made it past the first tier of palace steps. The man wore the official crest of Seraveth on his arm, his travel cloak stiff with road dust and dried mud and his hair plastered to his brow with sweat. One sleeve had been torn clean at the shoulder, as if someone had grabbed him and missed. His hands shook as he fumbled for the sealed parchment.

Rohannes did not make him climb any higher.

He took the letter with a practiced calm that did not match the sudden anxiety in his chest, broke the seal with his thumb, and read the first two lines.

He read it again, slower. As if a different pace might change the meaning. It didn't.

Rohannes looked up.

The palace courtyard was quiet in the early hour—only the faint clink of armor from guards shifting at their posts, the soft rush of the palace fountains, the first thin wash of sunlight turning marble pale gold.

He folded the parchment once, neatly, and gestured for the courier to sit on the lowest step.

"Water," he ordered a nearby guard. "Now."

The courier's knees buckled with relief. His eyes tracked every movement like an animal expecting a blow. Rohannes didn't waste time with comfort.

"You come from the border?" he asked.

The courier licked his lips, throat bobbing. "S—Sunspire," he managed.

Rohannes's jaw tightened. Sunspire was not a fortress city. It wasn't built for siege. It was a leftover relic from a time when Val-Or ruled the land. Its walls were old stone, its garrison light, its people traders and farmers who lived under the assumption that Seraveth's gold would shield them the way it always had.

Korvath had shown them what assumptions cost.

"How many survivors?" Rohannes asked.

The courier's gaze dropped. "I—I don't know. But...the smoke was visible for miles after I left. I've never run so fast..."

Rohannes closed his eyes for a single heartbeat. Then he straightened.

"Take him to the kitchens," he told the guard that brought water. "Feed him. Keep him within the lower wing until I return."

The guard hesitated, thrown by the sudden weight in Rohannes's voice. "Yes, Captain."

Rohannes turned toward the palace doors. He moved quickly, but never ran. Running belonged to panic. He was not permitted to panic in his station.

He went straight to Val-Theris.

The king's private office was lit from within, even at this hour. A thin line of pale light cut beneath the door. Rohannes raised his hand and pushed through the door without warning or formality.

Val-Theris stood at the tall window with his back half-turned, wings drawn close, hair unbound in the way he wore it only when he believed no one would see him. He appeared as though he was savoring the moments before he was forced to appear as a king again.

He turned when Rohannes entered, and something in his expression sharpened immediately. The Angelicus Prime did not waste time with preamble. He crossed the room and offered the folded parchment.

"News from Sunspire," he said.

His eyes went still as he read the letter. His face emptied. His wings closed quickly as if someone had wrapped a chain around them.

He read the letter twice as Rohannes had. Then, very slowly, he lowered it to the desk.

"They sacked one of my cities."

"Yes."

The silence that followed was sharp enough to cut.

Val-Theris turned away from the desk and stared at the window again. The sun had begun to crest the rooftops, bathing Solmiris in its false calm. The world looked too peaceful for the violence creeping closer.

Rohannes watched his king carefully. In the years he'd served him, he'd learned to recognize the small signs—how Val-Theris's fingers stilled when he was calculating, how his wings pulled closer when he was trying to hold something inside.

"Do you know if the garrison still stands?" Val-Theris asked quietly.

Rohannes swallowed. "Overrun. Whoever was present is either dead or fled toward another city."

"Summon the generals," he said. "All of them. Now."

Rohannes nodded. "Yes, Majesty."

"And send riders to patrol the borders," Val-Theris added.

"Korvath can cross anywhere. I want every inch of this kingdom fortified by nightfall."

Val-Theris reached for another parchment, ink already staining his fingers as if his body knew what was required before his mind had finished processing it.

Rohannes hesitated. Val-Theris's gave him a sharp look. "Speak."

"The council will use this," he said. "They will say this is the result of your attention diverted. They will say the refugees weakened our control. They will use Sunspire as proof that you have grown soft."

Val-Theris's eyes lifted slowly. "Do you truly believe that is any of my concern right now?" His gaze was dangerous in the morning light. "You have your orders. Make haste. I will inform the council that we are marching to Sunspire to purge the enemy from our lands. Korvath cannot be allowed to burn my cities and remain unpunished."

Then Val-Theris's eyes flicked toward the small side door— one that led down a corridor toward the guest rooms.

Toward Jesenia.

Rohannes followed the shift in his attention and understood immediately what would come next. "You should not go to her," he said gently.

Val-Theris's gaze snapped back to him. "Why?"

"Because she will ask you not to go," Rohannes replied quietly. "And you will want to obey her."

The king's jaw tightened. "She deserves to know," he said.

Rohannes nodded. "Yes. But you must be prepared to leave anyway."

"I am," he said.

He moved quickly then, crossing the room with a controlled urgency. His wings unfurled slightly as he walked, as if his body was already preparing for the air outside the city walls.

Jesenia's room smelled faintly of herbs and old books. The curtains were drawn back enough to let in pale morning light, which fell in soft bands across the floor.

Jesenia sat at the small table near the window, a blanket around her shoulders. A cup of tea sat untouched beside her, and in her hands was a dress she had been mending—thread caught between her fingers.

She looked up the moment he entered. Her expression shifted instantly, as if she'd learned to read him the way one reads weather.

"What happened?" she asked, voice already expecting hurt. She set the cloth down slowly, hands trembling faintly. "Val-Theris," she whispered. "Tell me."

"Korvath has crossed the border," he said. "They sacked Sunspire."

Jesenia went still. Her lips parted, but no sound came at first. Her breath hitched. "And you have to go," she whispered.

Val-Theris did not pretend otherwise.

"Yes," he said.

Silence. Her eyes filled with tears, fast and unwilling. But she offered him a sad smile. "I know." Jesenia shook her head, tears slipping down her cheeks before she could stop them.

Val-Theris's expression shifted, pain flickering across it. Her throat worked. She wiped at her cheeks roughly, angry at herself for weeping like this, angry that tears did nothing to stop armies.

"I do not want you to go," she said, voice cracking. "How do you know it will stop at Sunspire? What if it's a trap? What if this is Val-Oros trying to change you?"

Val-Theris's eyes held hers. "Because I have you. Because you remind me there are other ways to be strong. Because when I return, I want to be the man you can recognize."

Jesenia shook her head again, tears falling freely now.

"That's not fair," she whispered. "You shouldn't make your goodness my responsibility."

"You are not responsible for my goodness," he said gently. "You are the proof that goodness still exists in this world, despite it trying so hard to steal it from you."

Her eyes squeezed shut. A quiet sob broke from her chest, and when Val-Theris finally touched her, his hands settled lightly on her waist, steadying her as if she might fall apart. Jesenia's hands rose and gripped the front of his tunic, clutching him like a lifeline.

"I hate this," she whispered into him. She pulled back just enough to look up at Val-Theris, her lashes wet, her expression raw. "Promise me," she said, voice shaking. "Promise me you won't throw yourself into death just because you think it's inevitable. Promise me you'll fight to come back to me."

"I promise," he said.

Jesenia nodded once, as if anchoring herself to it.

Then her hands slid up to his face, palms warm against his cheeks. She held him there, looking at him as if she were trying to memorize every line.

"I don't believe in war," she whispered. "But I believe in you."

He leaned forward and pressed his forehead to hers. "I will return," he murmured. "Even if I have to tear the heavens to do it."

She kissed him then, hot and desperate. The kind of kiss that carried men through wars.

His hands slid down her arms, lingering at her wrists. He stepped back slowly, though the action broke something inside him. Jesenia's fingers clung to him for an extra moment before they fell away, empty.

He turned toward the door. Her voice stopped him.

"Val-Theris," she whispered.

He turned back. She stood now, shoulders squared despite her tears, shawl slipping slightly.

"Be safe," she said, the words simple and devastating.

Val-Theris's chest tightened. "I will be."

Jesenia shook her head, tears spilling again. "Don't say it like it's easy," she whispered. "Say it like you mean it."

Val-Theris held her gaze, then took a step closer to her once more, kissing her cheek. "I will come back to you."

Jesenia nodded, as if accepting it because she had no choice but to.

Val-Theris turned and left.

And Jesenia stood in the pale morning light, hands pressed to her mouth to hold in the sound of grief, watching the place where he had been as if staring hard enough might keep him within the walls.

By midday, the Golden City was no longer quiet.

Armor clanged in the lower courtyard. Horses screamed as they were saddled. Orders snapped through the air. Soldiers lined up in rows ready for direction.

Val-Theris stood at the head of them, wings unfurled wide, the sun catching along the edges until they looked like fire trapped in gold. Rohannes stood beside him, helm tucked under one arm.

The generals bowed, waiting.

Val-Theris's gaze swept over his men—faces young and old, hardened and frightened, all of them looking to him as if he could make the world make sense.

He lifted his hand, motioning toward the gates, and the city answered with the thunder of an army departing for war.

TWENTY-ONE

My Jesenia,

The eastern road is colder than I remembered. The wind cuts through armor as if it were cloth, and at night the fires burn low no matter how much wood we feed them. The men complain of the cold. I do not.

I have known colder things.

We reached the river pass at dawn yesterday. What remains of Sunspire is quiet now. Stone still smolders where flame kissed it last, and the air smells of wet ash and iron. I walked the streets myself. I made certain the wounded were tended before I ever accepted water or rest. You would have approved of the order in which I did things.

My men fight well. They are brave. They believe in what they protect. That belief carries them farther than steel ever could. Still, at night, when the camp settles and even the horses grow still, my thoughts wander somewhere warmer.

I find myself thinking of Solmiris at this hour—of the way the light catches the high windows just before dusk, turning the marble soft instead of blinding. I think of quiet rooms and open air and the sound of breathing not my own.

There are moments when the weight of command presses so heavily that I forget what it feels like to simply be. In those moments, I remember a voice that speaks without fear even when surrounded by those who wish it silent. I remember hands that mend rather than break.

There is a thought I carry into battle with me. A place I intend to return to. It is not marked on any map, nor defended by walls. It is simply...where I am most myself.

Know that I am unharmed. Know that I am careful, even when I do not appear so. I have kept my promise to you.

And know that every night I measure the distance between where I stand and where I wish to be.

Yours,

Val-Theris

Dearest Val-Theris,

The refugee quarter is restless in your absence, but not unkind. There are fewer arguments at the ration lines when your name is spoken aloud. It seems even those who do not know you understand that you are trying. I think that matters more than you realize.

I walk the same paths as before. I tend the same hands, soothe the same fevers, listen to the same griefs spoken only when no one else is near. Life continues because it must.

Still, I miss you most when the work is done and there is no one left to be brave for. I find myself listening for footsteps that do not come.

You spoke of returning to a place not marked on any map. I think I know it. I think it is the same place I go to when I need sanctuary.

Be careful with yourself, Val-Theris. I will not ask you to hurry back. I know better than to bargain with war. But my heart wishes for it all the same.

And when you return, I will be here.

Always,

Jesenia

MY JESENIA,

Today was not kind to us.

We lost too many before the sun reached its height. Good men—some young enough that they had barely tasted what life could offer. My men are tired. They fight because they must, because I ask it of them, because they believe in our nation and in me. But belief frays when the cost lies dead in front of them.

Tonight they look at me differently. They ask silently: Was this worth it?

I stood among them after dusk, listening to the wind move through our camp, and I realized something unsettling. I know how to command them. I know how to lead them into battle. But I do not always know how to carry them through the aftermath.

I find myself wishing you were here, because you understand grief without turning it into spectacle.

Tell me something, Jesenia. Something I can give them when duty feels like too much to ask.

With all my weary heart has to give,

Val-Theris

DEAREST VAL-THERIS,

Grief and suffering is not a failure of their strength. It is proof that what they loved mattered. Tell them that the dead do not measure that love by how loudly we suffer, but by how we choose to live afterward.

You carry them farther than you know, Val-Theris, and I believe that is because they look to you and see you standing among them. You don't ask of them what you are not willing to give yourself, and that makes you a soldier worth dying beside, not a king that demands they still stand while broken.

Always,

Jesenia

MY JESENIA,

I told the men what you said, and perhaps one day I can admit to them that it is your words that gave them strength that night.

In the days since, we moved on to the border where we found a company of Korvath's soldiers. We held the line at first light yesterday. Korvath's banners burned before noon. That should bring relief. Instead, it has given my thoughts too much room to wander. The men cheered when the smoke cleared, but I found myself unable to join them.

Instead, I thought of you, and of hands that know how to coax hope from wounded soil. I wondered what you would do with a place like this.

Oftentimes, my thoughts wander and betray my vigilance. Very unbecoming of a king, but I shall make the admission to you:

I wake sometimes with your name already on my tongue, after dreaming of running my fingers through your soft hair and the way my feathers tremble at your touch.

I am returning soon, and there is so much I want to say when I see you again. Things I have no courage for on paper. Things that belong to you alone, not to couriers and seals.

If fate is kind, I will say them to you myself before the next full moon.

Until then, know this: there is not a step I take that does not lean toward you.

I remain yours, more than duty allows me to confess,

Val-Theris

Dearest Val-Theris,

The people watch the gates more closely. They speak your name with something like faith, though I wish they would not place such a fragile thing in the hands of war. I fear my people are turning from their nature to reject such things. I have heard talk that what able-bodied men of Lunareth remain would defend Solmiris despite everything, because they continue to believe in you.

In the meantime, I try to be what they need. But when night comes and the lanterns dim, I allow myself the selfishness of imagining your return, and how warm my heart will be in your embrace.

I imagine your wings catching the light at the gates. I imagine the sound of your voice before I see your face. Sometimes I imagine nothing more than the weight of your presence nearby, enough to remind me that I am not alone.

Come back to me safely. That is all I ask. Should you return in the night after sleep has taken me, I beg you—wake me with the touch of your lips against mine.

Always,

Jesenia

TWENTY-TWO

THE CANDLES HAD BURNED LOW, pools of wax collecting at their bases. Jesenia sat curled in Val-Theris's private library, the same room that still smelled faintly of ink and sandalwood. For weeks she had come here every night, reading the histories he loved, surrounding herself with the ghosts of his voice and his handwriting.

Outside, the storm murmured against the stained-glass windows. She turned another page, the sound of parchment soft in the hush—then froze.

A floorboard creaked.

Jesenia's heart stuttered. The guards were never allowed this deep into the king's private wing. She glanced toward the shelves and, before thinking, gripped a heavy book in both hands. The moment another shadow slipped through the aisles, she swung.

A pale hand caught the spine in midair.

"Peace, my fierce scholar," Val-Theris said, laughing under his breath. "I leave for a few weeks and you arm yourself with literature. I thought you were a pacifist?"

Relief broke into laughter before she could stop it. The book slipped from her fingers and thudded softly to the carpet.

"I thought you would be at the border still," she said breathlessly before throwing herself into his warm, waiting arms.

He smiled—tired and beautiful. "I needed to see you before I had to be king again."

His kiss came hard and sudden, all the days of separation collapsing into a single heartbeat. Her hands tangled in his sweat-damp hair; his wings trembled open, enclosing her in warmth and the scent of him.

When they parted, he leaned his forehead against hers. "Korvath's soldiers are retreating for now," he murmured, voice low and rough.

Jesenia touched his cheek, tracing the faint bruise along his jaw. "You look like a man who has fought the sun itself."

He kissed her once more, softer this time, lingering. "I cannot stay long. I have much to do. But I could not bear another moment without seeing you."

Her hands rested over his heart, feeling its frantic rhythm. "Then savor this moment with me."

"I can give you more than that," he said. "Wait for me in my chambers. When I return, I will take you to our sanctuary where the stars are nearest. And there, Jesenia…" His voice deepened, promise threading through every syllable. "There I will love you until the heavens tire of watching."

He kissed her fingertips, one by one, then stepped back, his wings drawing close.

The door closed behind him with the hush of feathers, leaving the scent of rain and a heartbeat of silence. Jesenia pressed her hand to her lips, smiling through tears, and looked up toward the domed ceiling where the stars glimmered faintly through the glass—already waiting for them.

TWENTY-THREE

The library of Solmiris stretched in endless golden arches, the air thick with the scent of parchment and ink. The halls were silent at this late hour, save for the soft crackle of torches and the rustle of pages.

Val-Theris sat hunched over a long oak table, scrolls unrolled around him in neat, disciplined stacks. His fingers traced looping Lunarethian script, his lips moving soundlessly as he tried again to shape words not native to his tongue.

He had been this studious since he returned from the border and though the syllables were still clumsy, he pressed on, learning both the language and all he could of their courting rituals.

Here he learned that in Lunareth, lovers did not kneel before one another but stood side by side, facing the moon. That a man did not ask for a woman's hand with a ring like in Seraveth—he offered her a promise cloth, woven with his own hands, to show he would work for her comfort. This cloth was also part of a birthing ceremony, to be the first linen that touches the skin of a newborn as a blessing; for love would be the first thing they came in contact with. Marriage vows were not spoken to priests in Lunareth, but whispered under open sky where the stars themselves could hear. It was meant to be a private, intimate affair. It was a stark contrast to the lavish, public ceremonies they had adopted in his kingdom.

Val-Theris read every word, again and again, until the letters blurred. His fingers were smudged with ink from where he had traced their prayers, his hair falling into his eyes as he leaned closer to commit each fragment to memory.

Rohannes found him there once, long after midnight, his cloak draped over his shoulders, brows furrowed at the sight of his king muttering foreign words to himself.

"Your Majesty," he said gently, "Seraveth has traditions of its own. Would they not serve?"

Val-Theris did not look up, his voice soft but certain.

"Jesenia is not Seraveth," he murmured. "She should not be forced into my people's rites, certainly not after the way her and her people have been treated by mine. I have asked her once already, and she did not see it as an act of devotion. I shall not make that mistake again. When I ask her for eternity, it will be in her language, by her traditions, so there is no doubt it is *her* I love, not the idea of her."

He closed his eyes, whispering the vow once more under his breath, stumbling over the Lunarethian consonants but refusing to stop until the words came smoother.

And in that vast library, the Angel-King of Seraveth spent weeks devoting himself to learning how to love Jesenia properly.

As time went on, he became more comfortable with the words falling from his tongue, but with no one to practice speaking with, it kept him trapped in his studies for longer than he intended.

And of course, Jesenia began to notice.

The library was hushed as always, nothing but the sound of

wind from the open terrace fluttering through loose pages lining the shelves. Val-Theris stood deep in the aisles, a scroll of Lunareth Moon Prayer clutched in his hand, quietly whispering the words and simultaneously translating in his head.

At the end, he began fumbling the syllables, his voice growing louder at his own frustration.

He heard a soft laugh behind him, and turned to find Jesenia hiding in the shadows, her face laced with amusement. Her shawl was loose on her shoulders, and her hair fell down her back in soft waves. Her eyes glinted with mischief.

"You just said '*my life is your goat*'," she teased.

For the first time in his memory, Val-Theris felt the rise of embarrassment in his cheeks. "I…" His pale hair fell into his eyes as he fumbled to roll the parchment and put it away on a shelf. "It was not my intention."

Jesenia laughed softly and crossed the space between them, the light of a lantern above their heads warming her face. She placed her hands on his chest. "Perhaps not, but it was very charming."

"Charming?" he huffed, still embarrassed. He looked down at her, wings shifting awkwardly at his back, bumping against the rows of books. He thought it was a curse, the way his usual poise always crumbled under her gaze, but he did not care. His hands tenderly found her waist and pulled her closer. "Your language resists me after all these weeks of study."

"You've been studying my language? Why?"

"Because it is yours."

Her smile softened. "Well." She reached for the scroll once more, unfurling it. "Allow me to help, otherwise I fear you shall fill Solmiris with goats."

She led them to the table at the center of the library, placing the scroll between them as they sat side-by-side on the bench. Jesenia took Val-Theris's hand in hers and guided his fingers to trace the text as she repeated the phrases. Her voice was slow and clear, her accent gentle.

He followed along, a dutiful student trusting his tutor. Val-Theris let his free arm wrap around Jesenia, pulling her closer, sharing warmth. As they came to the last verse of the prayer, the air between them thickened into something deeper—charged with their closeness and so many unspoken words.

Val-Theris's eyes shifted downward to the shape of Jesenia's lips, and he could not resist leaning forward and touching them with his own. When they parted, he confidently repeated the line he had been trying to say before.

"My life is yours."

Jesenia smiled faintly against his lips. "There," she said lightly. "No goats."

His thumb circled lightly on her lower back, and he stared at the girl at his side like a lovesick fool, the corner of his mouth curled subtly, but certain.

IT WAS LATE, and the palace gardens were hushed beneath the silver wash of moonlight. The roses swayed faintly in the breeze, their petals glimmering like spilled stars. Jesenia stood among them, shawl pulled close, her eyes turned skyward.

"Jesenia," Val-Theris said softly, his voice low but sure.

She turned, surprised to see him. He had been distracted lately, busy with his duties. He stood before her without his cloak of state, without the guards or Rohannes at his side. Only himself, his golden hair catching the moonlight, and his wings folded close.

"I could not sleep." she said gently. He did not respond, but she could see it in his eyes that he came for her intentionally. He held out something folded carefully in his hands.

It was a strip of deep blue cloth, handwoven, uneven in its stitching but clearly labored over. The edges were frayed from where his fingers had worked it raw, but woven through its center was a pattern: Seraveth's golden thread knotted into Lunareth's crescent motif.

"Seraveth offers rings," Val-Theris said, his voice unsteady. "But Lunareth offers a promise cloth. I thought…" His pale eyes lifted to hers, raw and uncertain. "You deserve better than my politics, and I'm sorry I did not show you that before."

Her breath caught as she reached for the cloth, her fingers brushing his.

"You made this?" she whispered, feeling over the delicate stitching.

He nodded, wings shuddering faintly. "I honor you, Jesenia. Not as a queen to silence my council. Not as a refugee to soothe my guilt. But as the woman I cannot breathe without."

Tears welled in her eyes as she held the cloth against her heart, the fabric clutched in her hands.

"You are not my burden. You are my choice. My vow. My future," Val-Theris said, fierce and trembling. "I want to marry you with only the moon and stars as our witness, where my love for you is not some public spectacle to be judged by those blinded by prejudice. I want it to be yours and only yours." He stepped closer, his voice dropping to a whisper as he carefully pronounced her native language. *"My life is yours."*

This time, he spoke the words perfectly.

For a long moment, the garden was silent save for the rustle of roses in the wind. Jesenia's tears slipped freely now, but her smile was luminous.

"Yes," she whispered, her hand finding his, squeezing it. "Yes, Val-Theris. My life is yours."

He bowed his head, relief breaking across his features like dawn, and pressed his forehead to hers, his wings folding around them both as though to hide them from the watching world.

And for that one fragile moment, in the moonlit garden, the only thing that mattered was each other.

TWENTY-FOUR

The night was clear. The stars shimmered over Solmiris, spilling their silver light across the palace gardens. Roses swayed faintly in the night air, their scent heavy and sweet, carrying with it the hush of secrecy.

Jesenia stood among them, wrapped in a dress she had sewn herself from linen that Val-Theris had given to her in secret. It was simple, unadorned, and a deep blue. Moonlight clung to her shoulders, making her seem almost ethereal.

Val-Theris stepped toward her without the golden cloak and armor of his station only a simple red tunic, hair gleaming, wings folded low in humility. In his hands, he carried the promise cloth, blue and gold and silver threads woven into the Lunareth crescent.

There were no priests, no councilors, no crowd. Only Rohannes stood close by, keeping quiet vigil at the edge of the gardens, his eyes respectfully averted. Jesenia's heart thudded as Val-Theris stopped before her. His voice was soft, unsteady, but sure in intent.

"In Solmiris," he said, "they would demand we kneel before priest and crown. But I would rather stand here, with you. By the stars, Jesenia, I give you my vow."

He unfolded the cloth, wrapping it gently around their joined hands, binding them together in a ritual he had been studying for weeks. His eyes lifted to hers, luminous in the starlight.

"My life is yours, Jesenia," he whispered in her tongue, perfectly.

Tears welled in her eyes as she repeated the vow, her voice trembling but radiant.

"My life is yours, Val-Theris."

Their bound hands closed around themselves, fingers twining. Jesenia laid her free hand over his heart, feeling the strong, steady beat beneath her palm. "I am yours," she whispered again. "Not for Seraveth. Not for Lunareth. But for the man beneath the crown. For the heart beneath the wings."

He lowered his forehead to hers, the cloth binding them warm between their palms. "And I am yours," he breathed. "Not as king. Not as god. Only as a man who loves you."

They sealed their simple vows with a sacred, passionate kiss. His wings spread wide, folding around her like a canopy, as though even the stars themselves were not worthy to see her.

For that moment, there were only two souls, bound beneath the heavens. When they pulled back, Jesenia smiled through her tears. "We are wed. Husband and wife," she whispered.

"*Husband,*" he repeated. Val-Theris pressed his lips to her hand. "That is the only title I have ever earned."

When they retreated to his chambers, where he could love her properly as a husband upon soft sheets instead of cold marble, he promised that they belonged to no one but each other.

When he bent to kiss her, he was almost trembling. Jesenia's hands slid to his shoulders, then down to the strong lines of his back, feeling the faint tremor in his wings as they fluttered open slightly, like sails catching wind. She wrapped her legs around his waist and the night unfolded in tenderness: kisses pressed to collarbones and temples, hands wandering, laughter breaking softly between them when nerves tangled with desire.

After, Jesenia lay curled against his chest, her fingers idly combing through his pale hair as his wings folded protectively around them.

THE PALACE HAD GONE STILL for the night, as if it somehow knew the king needed it.

Rohannes stood at the end of the west hall, his back to a pair of gilded doors. Behind them, the king was not holding counsel or writing decrees. He was not discussing strategy or prophecy. He was doing something far more important: devoting himself to his wife.

After the ceremony, the Angelicus Prime felt it necessary to preserve their happiness just a bit longer, and so he stood guard long after his shift had ended.

He folded his arms across his chest, pretending to study the tapestry opposite him—a depiction of the Light of Val-Or. The angels carved into the threads all looked so solemn, so cold. But behind him beyond the privacy of the doors, he knew the angel was warm.

A guard from the lower ward came striding up the corridor, stopping short when he saw Rohannes stationed there.

"Captain," the man said, bowing stiffly. "I didn't know anyone was assigned to this post tonight."

"They aren't."

The guard hesitated. "Then—"

Rohannes leveled a look at him, calm but immovable. "Then you'll find somewhere else to be."

The soldier opened his mouth to protest, thought better of it, and turned away without another word. When the echo of his boots faded, Rohannes allowed himself a quiet sigh. He reached for the torch beside him, lowering the flame so it cast only the faintest glow.

Through the heavy doors came the sound of laughter.

Rohannes smiled to himself.

He had guarded this man through countless battles, watched him return bloodied and unbroken, had seen the light dim in his eyes after every vision of loss. But never, not once, had he heard his king *laugh*.

He leaned his shoulder against the wall, allowing his mind to rest for the first time in years. When the next patrol passed by, one of the younger guards nodded at him. "All quiet tonight, Captain?"

"All quiet," he said with a small, knowing smile. "Exactly as it should be."

MORNING LIGHT FELL soft and low through the halls, breaking into thin gold ribbons across the marble floors. The air was still damp from the night's rain, carrying the faint scent of cedar and jasmine from the gardens below.

Rohannes stood in the courtyard, arms folded behind his back, watching as the city below began to stir. Servants moved like ghosts through the halls, lighting braziers, drawing curtains, returning the world to order.

He heard footsteps behind him. Val-Theris appeared in the archway, robes loose, the faintest trace of sleep still softening his features. For once, the weight of his crown, literal or otherwise, was gone. He looked younger in the morning light, softened by the peace and serenity of the night before.

"Captain," he said quietly.

Rohannes turned, bowing his head. "Majesty."

They stood there for a moment, the sound of the fountain between them filling the silence.

"I hear you were stationed outside the west hall last night long after you were meant to return to the barracks for rest," Val-Theris said finally. Not a question.

Rohannes inclined his head. "I was."

A faint smile touched the king's lips. "And you heard nothing, I assume."

"Nothing worth reporting."

Val-Theris's expression softened. Something between amusement and gratitude flickering behind his eyes.

"You've kept my secrets, even the ones you shouldn't have."

Rohannes didn't look away. "Some secrets are worth keeping, Majesty."

The king studied him for a long moment. Then, in a rare gesture, he stepped closer and laid a hand on his shoulder. "You've given me many things in your service," he said quietly. "But last night, you gave me peace. That is no small gift."

Rohannes's throat tightened, though he kept his composure. "Every man deserves one night where the world can't find him."

Val-Theris nodded once, his eyes distant now, thoughtful. "Then I hope the world forgives me for wanting another." He turned to leave, the sunlight spilling over him as he crossed the courtyard.

Rohannes smiled to himself, shaking his head. "Foolish, impossible man," he murmured.

Val-Theris turned to throw a smile over his shoulder, but continued onward into the future he had so delicately carved for himself.

TWENTY-FIVE

Jesenia sat near the window of her chamber, the moonlight washing out her face as her hands folded low against her stomach. She had suspected for days—the weariness, the restless sleep, the faint morning sickness.

It should have been expected, the way they lost themselves in each other so often. But the only time they had discussed such things, Val-Theris was not even sure it was possible.

Tonight, after her missed blood, there was no more doubting.

When he entered the room, his steps softened at the sight of her stillness. His wings folded low as he crossed the chamber, kneeling before her where she sat.

"What troubles you?" he asked, his blue eyes searching hers.

She swallowed, then guided his hand to rest against her belly. "I think…" Her voice caught, tears welling in her tender eyes. "Val-Theris, I think we are no longer just two."

For a moment, he said nothing. His hand trembled against her, his eyes wide, his lips parting as if the air had fled him. For an instant, he forgot to breathe. His gaze lowered to her hand where it rested, then back to her face, her mouth trembling faintly as she waited.

"Jesenia," he whispered, his voice breaking on her name. "Are you sure?" As he asked the question, she began to sob, hiding her face in her hands. "My love," he said, unfolding her from herself, tenderly asking: "Why are you crying? This is wonderful news."

"They will hate this child before it even draws breath," she said through tears and heavy breaths. "This world will never be safe for them."

"That's not true," he whispered, pressing another kiss to her stomach. "I will reshape the earth to keep them safe. I swear it on all that is divine."

"I'm scared," she said, her mouth turning downward with sorrow. "I'm scared of the world we are giving them."

He threaded his fingers through hers, grounding her in the silent ways she had always grounded him as she threatened to spiral further into that fear. "Then I will change the world for you both if that's what it takes."

She brushed her trembling thumb across his cheek. "Are you…happy?"

He let out a sharp, unsteady breath—and then he bent, pressing his forehead to her stomach, his hair falling like a silky curtain around them both.

"Happy?" His voice cracked, shaking with something deeper. "I am undone. Jesenia, I am…I didn't even know such a thing was possible. It is a miracle. You are magnificent. You have given me more than I ever dreamed to ask. You have given me forever. That you would give your body, your strength, your heart, to carry something of mine…" He hesitated. "I do not deserve it."

Her breath caught at the rawness in his tone, and she turned fully toward him, cupping his jaw with one hand, thumb brushing lightly along the sharp line of his cheekbone. "It isn't about deserving," she whispered. "It's about *us*. About what we made together."

Val-Theris lowered his forehead against hers, eyes closing briefly as though grounding himself in her steadiness, her warmth, the quiet conviction she carried when his faltered. Jesenia leaned against him, her head resting lightly against his shoulder, the steady beat of his heart beneath her ear before reality struck her once more. She lifted her head from his and her eyes grew wet with fear again.

"Your vision…"

Val-Theris swallowed heavy. It was at the forefront of his mind too—his prophecy of death and the dread of knowing he was unable to escape it. He did not want to share that dread with her. Not now. So instead, he whispered:

"The future can change."

It was a lie.

Solmiris's high corridors were silent, lit only by the faint blue glow of lanterns lining the marble walls. Rain pattered softly against the towering stained glass windows, catching on the intricate carvings of Seraveth's winged saints.

Rohannes found Val-Theris where he often did when the weight of visions pressed hardest—standing alone at the eastern balcony, wings drawn close, his gaze fixed on the sleeping city below.

The gardens beneath were silver in the rain, gold-veined spires cutting against the clouded night.

"You called for me, sir," Rohannes said quietly, stepping into the cool wash of lamplight.

"Indeed," Val-Theris murmured, his voice soft but hoarse from silence.

"Something has changed in you." Rohannes moved closer, boots steady against the slick marble, until he stood a few paces behind him. "You've tripled the guard around the palace and the terraces without explanation."

Val-Theris's grip tightened on the carved railing, knuckles pale against gold-inlaid stone.

Rohannes waited. Val-Theris's wings shifted, feathers catching faint threads of lantern light. "It's about the unrest in Solmiris. In a way," he said with a particular sharpness, as though willing Rohannes to leave it at that.

"I know you better than that." His voice remained steady, low enough to keep the words beneath the veil of rain. "You can tell me."

The king said nothing for a long moment, his jaw squared and his eyes reflecting the restless lights of Solmiris below.

Finally, softly: "Jesenia carries my child."

The words hung in the cold air like fragile glass. Rohannes stilled, the sheer weight of those words holding them both frozen in place. "I see." He recovered quickly, as he always did, but his voice was lower now, edged with careful weight. "That is…dangerous knowledge, my king."

"I know."

"The council cannot learn of it." Rohannes's tone sharpened, footsteps drawing closer, the faint rasp of leather shifting as he rested a gloved hand against the railing. "You've seen how they already speak of her. Of her people. If they believe the bloodline of Solmiris will carry Lunareth in its veins—"

"They will not touch her," Val-Theris said flatly, his voice cutting like honed steel.

Rohannes's hand dropped back to his side. "I know you believe that. But you cannot fight them with words in this.

They will call for your abdication, or worse—civil war. They'll–"

"Rohannes."

For the first time, Val-Theris turned toward him, pale gaze bright beneath the shadows, his voice a whisper carrying too much weight.

"I've seen my death."

Something unreadable passed across the Angelicus Prime's face, his hands curling loosely at his sides, but he said nothing.

Val-Theris stepped forward, closing the distance until they stood shoulder to shoulder, his wings drawn wide enough to catch the lamplight, shadowing the space between them.

"I've seen it," he said again, softer now, almost a confession. "Blood on marble. My body broken beneath the throne. I thought I understood it and could accept it as destiny. But now…" His voice faltered, breath uneven. "Now all I can think of is Jesenia and our child. If I die, they'll be left alone in a city that wants them gone."

"You don't know that's what the visions mean for certain," Rohannes said, though his voice carried none of his usual surety.

"Yes I do," Val-Theris murmured, his gaze lowering to the sprawling lights of Solmiris below. "I feel it like I feel the air in my lungs and the heartbeat under my chest. This is not a fate I can escape."

Rohannes studied him for a long moment, reading the tension carried in every line of him—the king who was also a man, the angel who feared not his own death, but rather, losing the one tether still grounding him.

"I'll keep them safe," Rohannes said finally, voice low and steady. "Even if you fall, I swear it. I will take them from this city and find sanctuary far away from here where they cannot be harmed."

Val-Theris's jaw tightened. He could not ask that of

Rohannes, but neither could he bring himself to reject it. Neither spoke again. They stood together in silence, Solmiris's restless spires rising before them, the rain falling soft against his wings and the stone. And though neither said it, both men understood the same unspoken truth:

Destiny had already chosen where this would end, and Val-Theris would see it coming far too late to change it.

TWENTY-SIX

THE CHAMBER SMELLED FAINTLY of a soft rain. A brazier burned low in the corner, filling the room with gold light that shimmered against the marble. Jesenia sat near the fire, one hand resting lightly on her abdomen, the other nervously fraying the edge of her shawl.

The woman they'd summoned, Marise—one of the oldest Lunarethians and the last living midwife from the country—stood before them with her head bowed, her hands folded against her apron. Her skin was lined like dried riverbeds, her hair silver and braided with twine.

Rohannes stood near the door, silent and watchful. Val-Theris paced. When he finally spoke, his voice was quiet but sharp.

"You've delivered children before?"

Marise nodded, her voice rasping with age. "More than I can count, my lord. From mothers who had nothing left but faith and dirt."

"And they lived?"

"Most."

"*Most*," Val-Theris repeated, his tone clipped. "Most is not good enough for me."

"Nor to me, Majesty," she replied evenly. "But birth is not a thing men can command."

"Enough," Jesenia said softly, rising from her chair. "Val-Theris, please." She crossed the room and touched his arm. "This is Marise of Lunareth," she said, her voice gentler now. "I've known her since I was born. She brought half our village into the world, including me. She's never lost one without fighting the gods for it."

Marise inclined her head humbly. "I remember you, little Jesenia. Your mother would be very proud of the woman you've become."

Something in Val-Theris's expression flickered, that brief vulnerability only fear of fatherhood could summon. But still, his tone remained cool. "Do you understand what is at stake, Lady Marise?"

The midwife hesitated. "I do, my lord."

He stepped closer, the light from the brazier cutting across his features. "If word of this child reaches the wrong ears, the council will turn on her—and on your people. This is not simply a request for you to deliver this child, but to carry this secret."

Marise's voice was steady. "I understand."

"Then you will swear an oath of silence. You will tell no one what you see here—not your kin, not your gods."

The woman looked up at him, her eyes sharp despite her age. "You think I'd endanger her or her unborn child?"

Val-Theris stilled. "I am not a cruel man, but trust is not so easy to come by in my position."

A long silence followed. Rohannes shifted his weight, eyes flicking between them.

Finally, Jesenia spoke, her voice firm. "I trust her," she said to the king. "She is our only hope of ensuring this child is healthy while I carry them, and frankly, the only woman I'd trust to help me deliver."

Val-Theris turned to her, his face softening in the firelight. The fury that had simmered beneath his restraint ebbed into something closer to sorrow. "You know I would burn the world to keep you safe," he said.

"I know," she whispered. "But I do not want our child to be born into ashes."

Silence followed again, and Val-Theris approached her, placing a soft kiss to the crown of her head before his eyes settled once more on the midwife. "You will be compensated for your discretion."

Marise bowed her head. "You've been blessed, you know. Not by your Val-Or or your crown, but by her. The Light loves to pretend it makes miracles—but I've come to learn that sometimes miracles are just true love in disguise."

The king paused, the words catching him like a blade slipping between armor plates. He didn't answer—only inclined his head faintly before he escorted the woman out of the palace himself.

When the door shut behind him, Jesenia exhaled, sinking into her chair again, her hand instinctively finding her belly.

Rohannes lingered, studying her. "Forgive me for saying so, my lady," he said, "but I think you're the only person alive who can break through his stubbornness."

She smiled faintly, eyes tired but warm. "It's because he knows I don't speak to a king or a god. I speak to Val-Theris."

Rohannes nodded slowly. "Then keep doing so. The king listens to no one. But he..." He gave a small, rueful smile. "He listens to you."

With the midwife chosen, Val-Theris became a man filled with worry. Every time Jesenia moved, he looked at her with fear that she might break in half.

One day, during a long council session, Val-Theris observed Jesenia from the corner of his eye looking like she might be sick at any second. It was likely the cigars, or maybe even the scent of wine wafting toward her in the chamber.

He knew he was unable to ban those things from the chamber without rousing suspicion, so he sat helplessly throughout the session, physically restraining himself from reaching for his delicate wife by clenching his fists under the table.

When the session ended and the council chamber had finally emptied, Jesenia leaned against one of the carved columns, her hand pressed lightly against the curve of her stomach as she tried to steady her breathing. It had been just a sudden wave of dizziness and nausea, the kind that passed as quickly as it came—but the world still tilted faintly when she blinked.

"Jesenia."

She looked up, startled to find Val-Theris striding toward her, his cloak trailing across the marble. His wings were half-furled, feathers shifting as though unsettled by the change in the air itself.

"I'm fine," she said quickly, forcing a faint smile.

He stopped short in front of her, his gaze sharp, pale eyes searching her face as if reading something beneath her skin. His hand came up, cupping the side of her jaw gently, his thumb brushing along her cheekbone.

"You're pale," he murmured. "And your breath—"

"Val-Theris," she said softly, catching his wrist before his worry could spiral into command. "I just stood too quickly after we adjourned, that's all."

But he didn't seem to hear her. Without another word, he turned sharply toward Rohannes, posted near the archway. "Fetch the midwife. Now."

"My king—"

"*Now.*"

The word cracked like struck steel, leaving no room for hesitation. Jesenia exhaled slowly, closing her eyes for a moment as Val-Theris turned back to her, his hand hovering near her elbow but not touching, as though afraid she might splinter beneath his fingers.

"It isn't necessary," she murmured. "I just need to sit—"

He was already lowering her into one of the benches lining the chamber wall, his movements deliberate but unsteady with restrained panic. Kneeling in front of her, he pressed his palm against the curve of her stomach, gentle and reverent, his forehead lowering close enough that his hair brushed against her shawl.

"Please," he whispered, so soft she barely heard it. "Please don't do this to me."

Her breath caught at the sound—the naked fear, stripped of the king Seraveth demanded, the god he was born, and leaving only the man with a human heart and mortal fears beneath. She reached for him, her hand sliding into his hair, grounding him where he knelt before her.

"I'm not leaving you," Jesenia said softly, thumb brushing over his temple. "I am just tired."

His lashes lowered, the tension in his jaw intense enough to ache. "You don't know that."

When the midwife finally arrived, Val-Theris didn't move

from Jesenia's side, his hand locked around hers as though she might vanish into the silence if he let go. The examination was brief—Jesenia's pulse steady, her breathing calm, the child unharmed.

"It's normal, my king," the midwife said gently, bowing low. "Carrying takes its toll, and we cannot be sure if the child is more god than human. She needs rest, food, and less exhaustion from her councilor duties."

Jesenia gave him a small, faintly amused glance at that, but Val-Theris's expression remained unreadable, his gaze locked instead on the hand he still held in his.

When Marise left, Jesenia turned her free hand over to brush her fingertips against his knuckles. "See?" she said softly. "We're both fine."

Val-Theris lifted his head slowly, pale eyes burning with something deeper than worry now—something like defiance carved beneath quiet restraint.

"You are not fine," he murmured. "You're exhausted, surrounded by people who would rather see you gone, carrying the one thing in this world I cannot lose. I will not sit idle while you falter in front of them."

Her smile faded slightly at the weight in his voice, her thumb tracing over his hand in steady circles. "Then trust me to tell you when I need help," she whispered.

For a long moment, he didn't answer, his jaw still tight, shoulders drawn as though holding the world on his back. But when he finally leaned forward, pressing his lips softly to her forehead, the fight in him eased just enough to let her see the man beneath the king again.

"I will protect you whether you ask for it or not," he said quietly. "Even from the smallest breath of harm."

Jesenia rested her forehead against his, letting his promise settle into the silence between them.

TWENTY-SEVEN

Jesenia and Val-Theris walked the inner cloisters of the palace gardens, where the roses grew thickest and the fountains drowned out all other noise from the city.

Jesenia paused to steady herself near the fountain, her hand pressing instinctively to her stomach at a sudden wave of exhaustion and nausea. Val-Theris noticed at once, his brow furrowing as he reached for her elbow, his touch gentle but protective.

"You should not be walking so much," he said, his voice low, almost a gentle scold.

Jesenia smiled faintly, shaking her head. "If I sit too long, the child will think I am weak. And I will not raise a weak heart."

He stilled. For a moment, his eyes softened, and he bent to press a kiss against her hand. The gesture of a man whose world had narrowed to her and her alone.

"Come," she said. "This is important."

He followed her to the fountain where they mourned those lost in Lunareth together. Val-Theris helped Jesenia to the ground and sat cross-legged beside her, his wings folded loosely behind him. Between them rested a small, delicate paper lantern dipped in wax so it could float without soaking through.

"It's a Lunarethian tradition," Jesenia explained softly, tracing a fingertip along the rim of it. "When a child is expected, we set lanterns on the river to carry their names to good fortune. It's…a journal of sorts. A way to communicate with them beyond words. The river holds thousands of stories the mothers share with their babies. I've been told my own mother made hundreds when Danyel and I were in her belly." Her smile faltered briefly, but she steadied it.

He handed her the lantern and his fingers brushed hers briefly before lingering there. She looked up at him, startled, lips parting faintly before curving into a soft smile. Together, they lit the tiny wick inside, lowering the lantern into the rippling fountain that sat in the center of the palace's gardens.

Jesenia watched it with intensity, her thumb brushing the inside of Val-Theris's hand in a slow, unconscious rhythm. She leaned forward slightly, her voice lowering.

"My little one," she murmured, the words soft but sure, "this light is for you. It carries our hopes, not our fear." Her breath hitched faintly. "You come from a people who endured without becoming cruel. Who learned that mercy is not the absence of strength, but its truest form." Her hand pressed more firmly to her stomach, grounding herself in the warmth there. "I don't know what kind of world will greet you. I only know that I will teach you how to love it anyway."

Val-Theris's throat ached with emotions he had never felt before. He had faced battlefields without flinching, had watched cities burn in visions he could not change—but her words for their unborn child undid him in ways no prophecy ever had. He shifted closer, lowering his head until his forehead brushed Jesenia's temple. His voice, when he spoke, was uncharacteristically gentle.

"And I will teach you," he said, "how to carry what is heavy without letting it hollow you." His hand slid to rest over hers, over the curve of her stomach. "You will inherit a crown that was never meant to be a burden, but I fear it may become one for you. But you also inherit my vow—that you will never be alone beneath it. You are already braver than I am," he whispered, voice thick. "You exist without knowing fear or war or pain. I envy that innocence."

Jesenia turned her head slightly, her cheek brushing his shoulder. "You don't have to protect them from everything," she said. "Just teach them how to stand tall when the world tries to push them down."

The lantern reached the edge of the fountain, its light briefly reflecting in Val-Theris's eyes before slipping beyond the curve of stone and out of sight. Jesenia watched until it vanished, then leaned back against him fully, allowing herself the rare luxury of being held without fear of interruption.

Val-Theris wrapped his wings around them both, a pale arc of feathers closing like a sanctuary. He lowered his lips to her hair, breathing her in.

"Sleep well, little light," he murmured, not to the water, but to the life growing between them. Jesenia closed her eyes, her fingers tightening briefly around his. "We will see you soon."

As they were lost in their moment, neither of them noticed the servant boy carrying linens at the far edge of the cloister. He froze at the sight, eyes wide, the linens nearly slipping from his arms. He had seen enough: the King of Seraveth, his hand lingering on the belly of a refugee woman, a kiss pressed to her temple with tenderness that spoke louder than any proclamation.

By the time the boy reached the lower halls, his whisper had already spread. By nightfall, the palace was alive with it. Whispers slithered through kitchens, barracks, merchant halls. By the next dawn, the city hummed with the tale.

And by the third day, the council spoke of little else.

THE LAMPS BURNED LOW, their light pooling gold across the silk of the bed. Jesenia slept beside him, her breathing slow and even, the faintest rise and fall beneath the thin sheet marking the secret she now carried between them.

Val-Theris lay awake. He turned onto his side, watching her face in the candlelight.

Jesenia had never looked so peaceful. There was a soft warmth about her now, something he had no language for. Her hand rested loosely against her stomach, as though even in sleep she knew what she carried there and sought to protect it.

This was something he had believed impossible, but there it was, resting between them for him to admire.

He reached out, brushing a lock of hair from Jesenia's cheek. "Do you remember," he whispered, voice barely a sound, "the gardens?" Her eyelids fluttered but did not open. "You told me you wanted as many children as your body could carry." His throat ached. "I thought the Light had cursed me to rule, but not to create. That I was meant to guide life, never give it. And yet here you are, defying the divine again."

He pressed his lips to her hair, breathing her in. His voice trembled against her skin. "I'll give you as many as I can," he murmured. "As many as time allows before death finds me. You'll have a house full of laughter and noise and little hands tugging at your skirts. You'll have every dream you ever whispered to the wind, Jesenia." He exhaled slowly, eyes burning as his voice broke. "Even if I am not there to see it."

She stirred slightly. His hand tightened around hers. When sleep finally took him, he dreamed not of fire or ruin, but of sunlight and small voices calling his name.

And somewhere beyond the reach of dawn, the god who had made him watched, and said nothing.

THE COUNCIL CHAMBER was thick with the scent of incense, though it did little to mask the stench of whispered conspiracy. Councilor Gena leaned forward in her seat, her thin fingers steepled, her sharp eyes glinting like knives in the lamplight.

"It is confirmed," she said, her voice low, carrying across the chamber with deadly certainty. "We have watched her for two months. The Lunareth girl has missed her blood. She is with child."

Murmurs rippled through the chamber like a hiss of serpents.

Councilor Varin scowled, slamming a heavy hand against the marble table. "Then Solmiris's shame is doubled. The child within her is blasphemy carved into flesh."

"Not just blasphemy," Gena countered, her lips curving in a thin smile. "*Opportunity.*"

Several heads turned at that, uneasy. Gena rose, her long cloak trailing across the floor as she paced slowly. "The people already grow restless. They whisper of refugees draining our coffers, of weakness in the Angel-King who bends for foreign filth. This child will be the spark. All we need do is fan the flames."

One of the younger councilors shifted uneasily. "And if Val-Theris learns of our hand in it—"

"He need not learn," Gena cut in, her tone sharp as steel. "Rumor is a fire that requires no hand to guide it."

Varin's scowl deepened, though there was grudging agreement in his voice. "We must act quickly, then. The people will never kneel to a bastard heir."

"They will not need to," Gena said smoothly. "We will force his hand. Force him to choose: his crown…or his whore."

The chamber stilled at her words, the implication hanging heavy. At last, another councilor leaned forward, his eyes narrowing. "And what of the child?"

Gena's smile thinned further, cruel. *"Best it is never born."*

And though Val-Theris and Jesenia still slept peacefully in each other's arms that night, dreaming of names and futures, the first stones of ruin had already been laid beneath their feet.

Three days later, while Val-Theris was locked away in the war chamber discussing the situation at the border, Jesenia had been summoned by the Council without warning. Five guards came for her and escorted her through the dark corridors of the palace to a small room, where Councilors Varin and Gena waited.

"Lady Jesenia," Councilor Varin began smoothly, his voice measured, silk laid over steel. "We are grateful you have come."

"I wasn't aware it was optional," Jesenia replied softly, trying to hide in the folds of her shawl.

Varin smiled faintly, but it didn't reach his eyes. "We'll speak plainly, then. You carry the child of Solmiris's king."

The air in the chamber grew colder. Jesenia's heart stuttered, but she kept her expression steady. "I don't know what you're talking about."

"Do not lie, foreigner!" he snapped.

Gena, thin and sharp as a blade—leaned forward, her

knuckles resting against the wooden table between them. "That child will not inherit Solmiris's throne. Lunarethian blood will not stain Seraveth's crown."

Jesenia's breath caught, but she forced herself to meet Gena's gaze. "You have no right to accuse the king of such lies."

"We have every right," Varin interrupted, his voice steady and soft as falling ash. "The king does not govern alone. We have tolerated your presence because you kept small. But now, you have become dangerous."

The room fell silent except for Jesenia's ragged breathing.

Varin leaned back, folding his hands lightly in his lap. "Remove yourself from Seraveth before the child is born. Before your body shows our people this disgusting display of weakness," he said smoothly, his tone almost gentle now. "Or we cannot guarantee your safety. Nor theirs."

They said nothing more, and did not stop her as Jesenia backed out of the room with a panic she had never known. She retreated to Val-Theris's room, collapsing onto the chaise and muffling her sobs of fear with her hand.

What cruelty to threaten an innocent child.

There was no excuse for that evil, and Jesenia knew if she did not abide by their demands, they would not hesitate to make good on their threats.

When Val-Theris entered the chamber many hours later, he saw the look on her face. Unfocused. Fearful. Distant. He rushed to her immediately, his hair falling forward as he kneeled before her with all the concern of the heavens in his gaze.

Her name left his lips softly, but she flinched. "Tell me," he murmured, his voice low and steady despite the storm he felt building in his chest. "What is it? Are you in pain? Is the baby—"

"They know," she whispered, so quietly he barely heard her.

His grip grew firm around her hands. "Who knows what?"

"The council. About the baby." Her voice cracked, thin and

broken. "They said—" She faltered, swallowing hard before forcing the words out. "They said that I had to leave Seraveth before I began showing or else—"

"They *threatened* you?"

She nodded, breath shuddering, trying to steady her hands against his.

Val-Theris's chest rose sharply, once, as though the air itself had turned against him. Slowly, carefully, he lifted her chin, forcing her tear-bright gaze to meet his steady one.

"No one," he said dangerously, "threatens you. *No one.*"

"Please don't do anything that will make them hate us more," she begged, but Val-Theris could not grant her that wish—too blinded by fury and the desperation to protect his growing family.

THE COUNCIL CONVENED at dawn the next day by emergency order of the king. But only two councilors arrived, Varin and Gena, for they were the only ones to receive the summons.

In the gilded chamber beneath Solmiris's high dome, their murmured voices were already restless when Val-Theris entered.

"Your Majesty, what troubles you?" Varin asked smoothly, as if he didn't already know.

"You summoned Lady Jesenia without my knowledge." His voice cut through the chamber, quiet but unyielding. "You *threatened* the mother of my child," Val-Theris said evenly, though his wings flared faintly behind him, casting long shadows across the marble floor.

Gena rose, chin tilting defiantly. "We sought only to protect Solmiris's sovereignty."

"By promising the death of a woman and child?"

"She is no mere woman! She is the face of Seravath's weakness! We cannot allow it!"

Val-Theris stepped forward slowly, his eyes sharply cutting across the marble table like drawn blades. He stopped in front of Varin, his expression unreadable, his hands relaxed at his sides—and then, in a single, controlled movement, he drew a narrow dagger from its scabbard. Before anyone could speak, before Varin could even inhale, the blade slid clean and silent across his throat.

He collapsed soundlessly, blood spilling blackened red across the polished marble. Val-Theris looked down at him as if someone had spilled wine. Gena sat unmoved, but when the king's pale gaze met hers, the facade broke and fear shown in her eyes, her lips parting in silent horror.

"Let you both be a lesson to the rest of my Council. If any one of you ever so much as breathes her name again…it will be the last thing you do."

Then, his narrow blade met her throat as well. Gena fell limp to the table next to Varin's body.

Val-Theris turned sharply to the Angelicus Prime, who had been watching from the shadows. "Take care of them," he commanded, then strode from the chamber without another word, leaving the blood behind him.

While the Council dared not speak Jesenia's name again, they had already set plans into place that extended far beyond the deaths of Varin and Gena. The cost of their deaths was now etched into Solmiris's bones: the city would never forgive its king for spilling its own blood.

TWENTY-EIGHT

By nightfall, the markets of Solmiris were thick with whispers.

"The refugee carries the angel's bastard."

"They'll put Lunareth blood on our throne."

"Blasphemy. A curse on us all."

The words spread like rot, carried by merchants, servants, priests. By morning, graffiti marred the marble arches of Solmiris: crude smears of paint depicting broken wings, crowns cracked in half.

By the next morning, the unrest boiled over. Crowds filled the lower terraces, shouting, hurling stones at the *Hastati*, tearing banners from their poles. In the chaos, voices rose sharp and merciless:

"Down with the half-blood!"

"Purge the Lunareth filth!"

From the palace balcony, Val-Theris watched the riots churn like a sea of flame below. His wings snapped wide, his voice cutting across the roar.

"Disperse!"

For a heartbeat, the crowd stilled—and then came the reply,

ragged but unified, a chant that made Jesenia's stomach lurch even from inside the safety of the palace walls:

"No half-blood king! No half-blood heir!"

The last restraint in him broke.

He launched from the balcony, wings tearing the air, and landed in the heart of the terrace with the force of a falling star. The ground cracked beneath his boots, and the crowd scattered —but not far enough.

"On your knees," Val-Theris said softly, dangerously, his eyes burning. "Now." When they hesitated, he shouted once more. *"Now!"*

For a moment, it seemed as though they might obey.

The nearest rioters faltered, some sinking to their knees, others frozen mid-step with stones clutched uselessly in their hands. Val-Theris stood among them, wings flared, the light of his divinity cutting through the tension like a blade. His presence pressed down on them, demanding submission without another word.

Then someone laughed. It was sharp and nervous at first—an ugly sound that didn't belong in the silence. A man near the back of the crowd raised his voice, emboldened by the sheer number at his side.

"You hear that?" he shouted. "The angel defends his bed warmer!"

A stone flew with the words. It struck Val-Theris's shoulder and shattered against his armor, fragments skittering across the marble. Another followed. Then another.

Val-Theris moved before Rohannes could reach him. His wings snapped outward in fury. The air screamed as he surged forward, the force of his passage knocking men flat where they stood. He seized the man who had spoken first by the front of his tunic and lifted him clear off the ground.

"You forget, I am your king," Val-Theris said, his voice low and terrible, each word trembling with barely leashed violence.

The man choked, clawing uselessly at Val-Theris's wrist, then spit in his direction. He dodged the spittle. Around them, the crowd surged again, panic overtaking bravado as the loyal *Hastati* charged in at last, shields raised, blades flashing.

Val-Theris hurled the man aside as though he weighed nothing. He turned, eyes blazing, and raised one blood-slicked hand.

"Drive them back," he commanded, his voice ringing like a death knell. "Make them remember who I am."

Feathers cut through the smoke like blades. His soldiers followed his fury, striking hard, scattering rioters with merciless precision. Screams tore through the terraces, the sound of bones breaking against marble. The people who had once chanted his name now fled from him in terror.

From the high windows of Solmiris, Jesenia pressed her hands against the cold stones, her heart hammering as she watched the chaos below.

And in the middle of it all, Val-Theris stood unyielding, his wings spread wide, blood on his feathers, his hand slick with the proof of violence.

Jesenia's hand went to her stomach, tears breaking down her face "This isn't what I asked for," she whispered to the silence. "Not this."

When Val-Theris returned to their chambers, his cloak was torn, his hands bloodied. He reached for her at once, his voice soft, almost tender.

"They will not threaten you again," he whispered, as though his brutality were a gift. "The city has been reminded who their king is. It is by my rule they live such lavish lives, and they will do well to remember that. They will never dare speak against our child again."

Jesenia stepped back before he could reach her, her tears still streaking her cheeks and her hand trembling faintly where it rested protectively over her stomach. The movement struck him harder than any blade.

"At what cost, Val-Theris?" she asked, her voice breaking. "You said you would protect us. But all I see is more blood. More hate. You're giving them reason to despise us. To despise me. How can this save our child? They will never forgive me for what you've done in my name."

Val-Theris's wings shuddered faintly as though from an unseen weight—perhaps even guilt. "I did what I had to do," he said, though the words sounded more like a plea than conviction.

"Every drop of blood you spilled makes the whispers louder. Every scream you silenced becomes another curse upon our child."

"You don't understand," he whispered. "If I let things worsen they will take you from me. I cannot let that happen."

"And if you keep going?" Jesenia asked, her voice trembling. "What will be left of you when our child comes into this world? Will they inherit a father? Or a tyrant who calls himself angel?" Her voice cracked then, and she turned away, her shoulders shaking as she pressed her forehead against the cold stone wall. "I can endure your people's hatred," she whispered. "But I will not raise this child in blood. If you cannot stop this path…then perhaps I was not meant to stay."

Val-Theris stood frozen, his wings half-furled, his hands clenched helplessly at his sides.

"Jesenia," he said finally, softly, his voice raw. "Don't ask me to choose between you and my crown. Because you know I will choose you. Every time."

But when he reached for her again, she didn't move. She

stood trembling, her hand pressed to her stomach, and Jesenia realized that the man she loved was vanishing beneath his fear—and the child she carried would be born into a kingdom drenched in blood.

220

TWENTY-NINE

With Jesenia distraught at his actions, Val-Theris thought it best to give her space to breathe. For all the lengths he would go to keep her safe, he never wanted to upset her by doing so.

He found himself once again in the Hall of Radiance before the carving of Val-Or. It had been months since he had last spoken to his father, or at least tried to.

Val-Theris took a deep, exhausted breath. "I need you," he begged to the carving. When there was no answer, his mouth twitched into a scowl, and his fist met the stone with a resonating crack.

The moment his fist collided with the wall, a blinding flash of light broke free from the fractures. When his vision focused once more, he was surrounded by…nothing.

There was no pain like his prophetic visions, and his mind felt clear.

He stood barefoot in a himation. Upon his exposed chest, a marking in the shape of a sun blazed from under his skin. He was in a plane of pale light that stretched endlessly in all directions, neither warm nor cold, neither solid nor void. Above him, the heavens unfolded in layered expanse—veils of luminosity drifting like slow-moving clouds, threaded with faint constellations that did not belong to any sky he knew.

Val-Theris did not move.

"You have come," a voice said. It existed everywhere at once, folded into the light itself. Val-Theris searched for the speaker, but he saw nothing at first.

Then, the light ahead of him gathered, condensing into form—not flesh, not quite, but the suggestion of it. Wings took shape first: one of gilded feathers, one of brilliant flame. Then the suggestion of a body, tall and indistinct, robed in brilliance that shifted as though refusing to settle.

Val-Theris kneeled with unwavering respect for the man before him.

"Father."

"You honor me still," Val-Or said. "Even after all this time." If he smiled, it was only a soft alteration in the light. "You have not changed, my son."

Val-Theris felt the enormity of the place press against his wings, against the years of questions he had carried without answers.

"Why did you bring me here?" he finally asked. It was quiet for a moment, and then Val-Or spoke once more.

"Will you not look at me?"

Val-Theris lifted his head, and the light dimmed slightly, allowing him to look upon his father in…he didn't even know how long. Maybe the first time ever, for he had no clear memories of him. When his gaze settled, he noticed a thick tie of cloth across Val-Or's eyes.

Val-Theris furrowed his brow in confusion. "Father—"

"It is why I gave my sons the gift of prophecy," he answered without needing to hear the question. "For I ruled blindly. I tried to be a benevolent god, but I could not see where my choices would lead. When the world began to resist my Light, I gave it my sons, to see where I had been blind."

Val-Theris folded his wings closer to his back and finally stood. "You gave the burden to us."

"I gave you *sight*," Val-Or replied. "Sight is not a burden, Val-Theris. It is a tool. One I hoped would allow you to succeed where I could not."

"And Val-Oros?" Val-Theris asked.

"He was given a narrower gift," his father said. "He sees what *touches* fate. You see what *follows* it."

Val-Theris exhaled slowly. "And which of us did you intend to rule better? If Val-Oros is your answer, then he is your greatest failure."

Val-Or did not answer immediately. "When I created you," he said at last, "I did not intend either of you to rule above one another, but together. You were meant to *balance*," Val-Or continued. "Two opposing truths. Flame and mercy. Consequence and restraint. I believed the world could survive my absence if the two of you held it together."

Val-Theris's jaw tightened. "Instead, he rules with terror."

"Yes."

"And I rule with hesitation."

"Yes."

Another silence.

"You see what he has become, yet you do nothing to stop it," Val-Theris said.

"I have seen what he *is*," Val-Or replied. "And what you will be forced to do. Tis not my place to interfere. I no longer have such power." Val-Theris's wings shuddered faintly. Val-Or's light dimmed further. "You will kill him, and he will return to me to face his judgement."

Val-Theris closed his eyes. "I have already seen that," he said quietly.

"Not as clearly as you think."

Val-Theris opened his eyes again. "Then tell me, *please*," he begged. "For once, help me understand what I see."

Val-Or's form shifted, and suddenly the heavens around them changed.

Val-Theris saw Seraveth—not as it was, but as it would be. Walls fractured. Gold blackened by smoke. Banners torn and trampled beneath fleeing bodies. He saw wings folded in grief at the center of it all.

And he saw Jesenia kneeling amid ruin with a full womb, crying. His breath caught.

"You know what she carries," Val-Theris said gently.

"I do. She carries life shaped from both of you," Val-Or continued. "God and mortal, a union I never saw."

"But I don't understand. Val-Oros—"

"Has not the capacity to love as a father should love. The Light can see what is in your hearts, and it has blessed you as it will never bless him."

Val-Theris stepped forward instinctively. "Then tell me how to protect them after I'm gone."

Val-Or did not move. "*After you're gone*," he repeated quietly. Then, he simply said: "I cannot."

Anger flickered in Val-Theris's eyes. "Do not tell me you brought me here simply to explain my suffering instead of easing it. After all these years of me begging for your guidance, that is what you give me?"

"Yes."

Val-Theris straightened, wings flaring just enough to catch the light. "Then tell me this: does she truly undo my kingdom as Val-Oros saw?"

Val-Or regarded him for a long moment.

"She does not undo it," he said at last.

Val-Theris closed his eyes again with relief. "Then what of

my death? Is there nothing I can do? Must her and I truly suffer through this knowing our child will one day be fatherless?"

"Death will come for your family," Val-Or confirmed. "It is known. It is final."

"Can I know how long I have left? Will I get to hold my child?"

Val-Or thought for a while, as if debating if that knowledge would throw off the balance of the universe.

"I will only answer one of those questions. You must determine which is more important to you."

Val-Theris took a deep breath. "Please, tell me I get to hold my child at least once."

Val-Or went quiet again, before he solemnly said: "No."

A shudder wrecked through Val-Theris's body, and tears escaped his eyes. "Is the Light really so cruel?" he asked through a sob.

The heavens began to dissolve.

"Wait! Father," Val-Theris said quickly. "I have more questions. Please."

But the light vanished.

Val-Theris woke on the floor of the Hall of Radiance with hot tears on his face and an unfathomable pain in his heart, shaped by the crushing certainty that the future had finally stopped hiding from him.

THIRTY

The chambers were quiet, the city beyond their windows restless beneath Solmiris's starlight. The soft perfume of night-blooming jasmine drifted in from the gardens below, mingling faintly with the lingering warmth of burning oil lamps.

Jesenia sat curled on the velvet bench beside the carved window, her shawl slipping loosely from one shoulder. The moonlight caught the silver threads in its fabric, scattering faint glimmers across her skin. One hand rested lightly against her abdomen, absentminded and protective.

They had spoken little since he spilled blood in the streets for her. The guilt weighed heavy on her shoulders as if she were the one who drew the blade herself. It made her more sick than usual, and Val-Theris could see the way his actions affected her.

He stood at the balcony doors, leaning against the carved stone frame, his wings drawn close to his back. His gaze had been on the city for some time, tracing the faint flicker of distant torches where the lower terraces still churned with unease. But none of that mattered to him now. After his conversation with his father, he couldn't find it in himself to care about anything at all, save for Jesenia and their unborn child.

She gasped softly. It was a small, startled sound that made him turn instantly, his pale eyes sharp beneath the dim glow of the chamber lamps. She was staring down at her hand, fingers pressed gently against her stomach, wide-eyed.

"Jesenia?"

Her breath trembled. "I felt them move," she whispered, her voice soft with awe. "Val-Theris, I felt it!"

He crossed the room quickly but quietly, as though afraid to disturb something sacred, kneeling before her without a word. His hand hovered in the space between them, hesitant to touch until she caught it and guided him gently, placing his palm over the soft curve of her stomach.

They waited in silence.

And then he felt the faint fluttering, fragile as the brush of a moth's wing. Val-Theris stilled completely, his breath catching, every trace of tension drawn taut beneath his skin. He bowed his head, his hair falling forward to brush against her shawl, his voice breaking the stillness.

"There is life," he whispered, reverent and disbelieving.

Jesenia smiled faintly, everything she had felt the days prior fading away, her free hand brushing across his temple. "That is our future," she corrected gently, tears gathering at the corners of her lashes.

Val-Theris looked up at her then, and for a heartbeat Jesenia thought he might shatter—there was too much in his gaze, a thousand unspoken things pressing behind his pale eyes. He reached up, cupping her jaw carefully, his thumb sweeping against her cheek as though memorizing the shape of her face in this exact moment.

He kissed her then. Soft at first, then deeper, the restrained edge of someone who carries both love and desperation in equal measure. Her fingers tangled lightly in the collar of his tunic, pulling him closer as his wings shifted behind him, arching slightly, shadow stretching against marble and lamplight.

It lasted only a moment, but when they parted, his forehead pressed gently against hers, and she caught the tremor in his breath.

"You're afraid," Jesenia whispered.

Val-Theris closed his eyes, swallowing against the weight in his chest. "Every day."

Jesenia brushed her thumb along his cheekbone, steady where he faltered. "Then hold onto us," she said softly. "Whatever comes, we meet it together. As one."

For a long moment, he simply held her, one hand still pressed gently against her stomach, as though trying to anchor himself to the faint flutter of life beneath his palm.

Neither of them knew this would be one of the last nights they'd ever dream of names, of soft mornings, of futures built in the soft light of their love.

Soon, Solmiris would take everything from them.

Of the ninety-three Lunarethians that arrived at Solmiris's gates, eighty-three remained.

Of the ten that were lost, among them, the last two living infants that were born before Lunareth fell were lost to fever. This knowledge weighed on Jesenia daily now. She carried the future of her country inside her. Though she was overjoyed, and Val-Theris called it honorable, she could not help but feel guilty for it. She suspected she was the only woman of birthing age from Lunareth that was healthy enough to conceive. Due to her time at the palace during late council sessions and her secret marriage to the king, she had once again filled out and held the curves she was born with.

All the while, her people still had to beg for scraps.

Jesenia moved through the refugee quarter with practiced familiarity, though it had been days since she last came. Smoke rose in soft plumes from low hearths and shared ovens, curling around patched linens and salvaged stones.

Her shawl was drawn close, though the morning was mild, her steps measured as she navigated uneven cobblestone. People noticed her at once. They always did now. Some bowed their heads. Others pressed hands to their hearts. A few reached out—not to touch her, but to brush fingers against the hem of her sleeve as she passed, as though proximity alone might offer reassurance that she was both there and still working to improve their conditions.

"Lady Jesenia," someone murmured.

"Blessings," said another.

She answered them softly, nodding, pausing when she could, though the weight of their attention pressed heavier than usual today. Desperate, almost painful in its intensity.

She turned down a narrower lane where the stone darkened with age and dampness. At the end of the lane stood a makeshift tent, painted with a simple symbol of a crescent moon. She stopped before it, resting her palm briefly outside as she steadied her breath and peeked inside.

"Come in," came a voice from within, low and steady. Jesenia smiled faintly and pushed the linen open.

Marise sat inside atop a pile of hay and dried leaves. Her hair, once black as obsidian, had faded to silver, braided and bound at the nape of her neck. Her hands were strong and sure, stained faintly with ink and herbs, her eyes sharp with a kindness that did not dull with time.

"There you are," Marise said, setting aside a bowl of steeping leaves. "I was beginning to worry that palace had swallowed you whole."

"Not yet," Jesenia replied gently. "Though it's tried."

Marise gestured for her to sit, then her gaze dropped at once to Jesenia's stomach, her expression softening.

"You carry yourself differently," she murmured.

Jesenia lowered herself carefully onto the cushions. "I *feel* different," she admitted. "As if I'm carrying my fear in my stomach instead of my child."

Marise approached slowly, achy knees cracking as she moved closer. She placed both hands gently against Jesenia's stomach, eyes closing as she bowed her head.

"Ah," she breathed. "There you are, little river."

Jesenia's breath paused.

Marise opened her eyes and looked up at her. "They will be large and healthy, I think. Fitting for the child of a god, hm?" She listened once more. "The spirit of this little one is strong. They press outward, even now."

"That's good?" Jesenia asked quietly.

"It means they will not easily cower to the struggles of this world," she replied. "What of your sickness?"

"Only worse at the smell of meat. I think this babe will be grown on bread alone."

Marise smiled at that. "The baby will tell you what it wants. If that is bread, then I would give all of my grain to you."

Jesenia swallowed. "Don't say such things."

"But it's true," Marise said. "I am old now. I have lived a full life. I have loved. I have lost. I have experienced boundless joy and endless sorrow. I have brought many lives into this world, but I suspect this one may be my last. My dying wish is for this child to play in Lunareth's river before their world grows bleak. This child is a miracle; you carry proof that love was not lost when our homes fell. Promise me, no—promise *Lunareth*, Jesenia, that this child will know the strength it came from."

Jesenia sobbed and wiped her face with her sleeve. "Yes. Yes, I promise—"

As she spoke, a distant, loud, hollow boom vibrated through the stones beneath them. The two women stood together and stepped out of the tent. The conversations in the street faltered and the refugees searched for the source of the sound.

Another boom followed, closer this time.

Then the bells began to ring. The frantic, uneven toll reserved for only one thing.

Invaders.

Shouts rose from the direction of the gates. People surged instinctively toward shelter, fear cracking through the fragile calm like ice splitting underfoot.

"Korvath!" A *Hastati* above them screamed. "Korvath at the gates!"

As he finished his warning, he went limp, falling from the top of the wall and crashing to the refugee quarter below with an arrow lodged precisely in the gap between his plated armor and his helmet.

Jesenia turned from the sight, her breath caught in her throat as smoke rose in the distance, dark against the sky. The ground seemed to shudder beneath her, as if the city itself recoiled from what approached.

Her hand flew to her stomach, instinct overriding thought. The quarter erupted into chaos—children crying, elders shouting instructions, men scrambling to form lines and grab any weapons they could find. Stones. Sticks. One man even pulled the arrow from the fallen soldier and held it like a javelin.

"Go," Marise said sharply as she shook Jesenia. "Back to the palace. Now."

She couldn't argue. She tried to turn and run, but as she did,

Korvath's soldiers broke through the front gates of the city, swiftly cutting off any escape. Something slammed into her from behind, rough hands yanking her backward into the crush of bodies. A hand clamped over her mouth before she could scream, her shawl torn as she struggled, breath ragged and sharp against her captor's gauntlet.

They cut men down where they stood, and any women they could grab, they did, corralling them like cattle at the central plaza of the city.

Among them, was Jesenia.

THIRTY-ONE

THE FIRST HORNS split the silence like a blade. They did not sound like the ceremonial calls Solmiris had grown accustomed to in his time as king—the measured notes of assembly or triumph—but a warning torn from lungs already burning with fear. The sound reverberated through stone, rattling the banners that hung along the high walls of the palace and setting every nerve in his body on edge.

Val-Theris was in the war room when the Angelicus Prime burst inside, his face pale beneath streaks of blood.

The ministers and generals inside startled. A few hands went instinctively to their weapons, but relaxed when they saw Rohannes. But he was disheveled—worried. His cloak was torn. One gauntlet was missing. Blood streaked across the edge of his jaw where a blade had kissed him.

Rohannes had always been composed, even in battle. Even when death pressed close enough to whisper. To see him like this —armor scarred, breath uneven, eyes burning with urgency— sent a ripple of unease through the room.

"My king, Korvath has breached the main gate."

A cold weight settled beneath Val-Theris's ribs. But then his posture changed into that of a seasoned soldier. Fearless. Prepared. He hastily stepped with Rohannes toward the doors and out the palace.

"Mobilize every *Hastati* soldier in this city," he ordered, his voice clipped and sharp. As they passed through the palace doors, a fresh gust of wind drove thick, bitter smoke into their faces. Below, the city roared with fear. Warning bells rang. Steel struck steel. Screams rose and fell.

"Val-Theris," Rohannes said, turning the king's attention directly to him. There was something urgent in his voice that had not been there moments before. The kind of urgency that preceded words that would change everything. "They've taken hostages."

By the time Val-Theris and the *Hastati* with him reached the plaza, the air was thick with smoke and tension. His soldiers formed a hard line behind him, halberds raised, their feathered plumes dulled by ash and sweat, but the enemy stood firm in the center—and between them, the hostages knelt, hands bound, faces ghostly with terror.

The plaza had once been a place of commerce and ceremony. Now it was scarred beyond recognition. Fires burned unchecked along the edges, devouring market stalls and tapestries alike. Shattered stone littered the ground, slick with blood that reflected the flames in dull, trembling pools. The air rang with the sound of crackling wood and distant screams, punctuated by the sharp bark of Korvathian commands.

It was only women and children kneeling, as if they were the only target of this attack. If any of them cried too loudly, Korvath's soldiers cut them down. Something caught Val-Theris's eyes at the very center of the group—two young children crying near what could only be assumed to be their dead mother.

The woman lay slumped forward, her body shielding nothing now, her hair matted dark against the stone. One of the children clutched at her sleeve, shaking her as though she might still wake. The other sobbed openly, face streaked with soot and tears, their small shoulders hitching with each breath.

Val-Oros landed in front of them then, his flaming wings shooting outward. The heat of his descent rippled across the plaza, forcing even his own men to step back. Stone blackened beneath his boots, cracks spiderwebbing outward as if the ground itself recoiled from his presence. He turned to the crying children with a scold on his face.

"Be quiet!" He barked, but the children only cried harder.

And the sight that followed made Val-Theris go still with dread. Jesenia, kneeling among the hostages. She had reached for the two children and wrapped her shawl around their faces so they did not see the blood.

"You again?" Val-Oros said, grabbing her roughly by the arm. When he did, his eyes glossed over with his prophetic vision.

He saw this Lunarethian girl lying on a chaise with his brother at her back, their hands resting lightly over her stomach. Intimacy. Tenderness. A future he would never let his brother taste.

The vision left him as quickly as it came, and Val-Oros decided in that moment that this would be the way he would break his brother and put an end to this war.

Val-Theris's wings twitched instinctively to take flight—to go to her, but he forced them still as his gaze locked on the curve of her face and the strands of hair knocked loose from her braid.

Every instinct screamed at him to abandon formation, to damn the consequences and tear the plaza apart stone by stone until she was free. He tasted blood where his teeth cut into his lip, the discipline that had ruled him for centuries fraying under the weight of her presence there.

And because the world's cruelty knew no end, Jesenia's eyes landed on him just enough to make his chest splinter, and Val-Oros noticed.

"Well, well," Val-Oros said, his voice carrying easily over the square, laced with cruel amusement. "The rumors were true, then. The Angel-King and his little foreign pet."

A ripple of laughter broke through the enemy's ranks.

Val-Theris's jaw tightened, his voice low and even despite the icy fire beneath it. "Let her go."

His voice came out far weaker and more desperate than he had meant it to.

"Oh, we'll let them all go," Val-Oros said lightly, waving vaguely at the kneeling hostages. "Refugees, citizens, children. We're merciful like that."

Around them, Korvathian soldiers laughed softly, the sound harsh and metallic beneath the crackle of nearby fires. One man nudged another with his elbow, nodding toward the bound figures as though they were livestock at auction rather than lives held in the balance.

He pulled Jesenia to her feet by her hair and forced her forward, closer to where Val-Theris, Rohannes, and the *Hastati* formed a line. He then jerked her head slightly so her face tilted toward Val-Theris. She gritted her teeth to keep from crying out at the sharp pain at her skull.

Her braid came loose in his fist, strands tearing free as her knees stumbled against the uneven stone. Dust clung to her palms where she caught herself, her breath coming short and shallow. The distance between her and Val-Theris felt suddenly unbearable—only a few strides apart, yet bridged by blades, fire, and a brother's cruelty.

He stopped abruptly, turning his gaze back to Val-Theris, his voice dropping sharp. "All you have to do is kneel before your king."

No one dared move. Not until Val-Oros drew a sharp dagger from his belt and flashed it tauntingly at his brother. Val-Theris took a step forward.

The blade pressed against Jesenia's neck threateningly. "Ah-ah!" Val-Oros mocked. "One step closer and your heir dies before it draws breath."

The cold edge bit into her skin, and she gasped despite herself, tears blurring her vision as fear surged hot and wild through her veins. The threat hung there, obscene and absolute, spoken loud enough for every soul in the plaza to hear. A bead of bright blood was pressed out of her skin, and her panicked breath came ragged, her pulse hammering in her throat. "Please," she begged her captor, but Val-Oros wasn't listening. He had his eyes locked on Val-Theris, who was frozen in fear for Jesenia and their child.

Jesenia's arms wrapped around her middle, clutching instinctively against her stomach. The silence of the plaza was suffocating.

Val-Theris repeated her pleas. "Please," he begged his brother, hoping something inside him still yearned to give mercy. "I'll give you what you want. Just don't hurt her."

His voice broke on the final word, stripped of command and divinity alike.

Val-Oros chuckled low, sharp and cruel "I told you what I want. I want you to *kneel* before your *king*. I want your city here as witness as you trade your divinity for a woman."

He spread his free hand toward the plaza, toward the shattered streets and watching crowds, savoring the weight of every eye upon them. This was not merely conquest; it was spectacle.

And for the first time in history, Val-Theris kneeled before another in submission. He did not hesitate this time. His wings folded low against the ground, and his eyes never left Jesenia's. "Please, King Val-Oros, have mercy on my wife and child."

Murmurs echoed through the plaza. Now everyone knew how far Val-Theris's devotion to the Lunarethian girl went, a secret only Rohannes knew before. The three kingdoms of the realm watched the eternal, untouchable Angel-King of Seraveth *beg*.

Val-Oros grumbled in satisfaction. His smile was slow and indulgent, the smile of a man who had waited lifetimes for this moment. "Good. Now the world sees what a god hides beneath his feathers."

With a sharp gesture, Val-Oros pushed Jesenia to the ground in front of Val-Theris, who barely caught her before her stomach touched the stones. His hands instantly cradled her with desperate care as though his body knew before his mind that she must be shielded at all costs.

With Jesenia out of the hands of Korvath's soldiers and its king, Val-Theris's eyes sharpened into something deadly.

"Burn them all," he commanded his *Hastati*. "I want every soldier of Korvath reduced to ashes."

The words rang out across the plaza, sharp and absolute, the same words that had once sent armies scattering and cities falling silent beneath his shadow. Smoke curled around his wings as he spoke, the air still thick with the scent of blood and scorched stone.

The *Hastati* had once knelt at the sound of his wings. Now they stood in silence, ranks unbroken, shields grounded, spears upright but unmoving.

Val-Theris faced them. He gave the order calmly, as he always had.

"*Advance*. Give no quarter for Korvath's men."

The command echoed and died. The plaza answered him with nothing but the crackle of burning debris and the distant sob of a wounded child. No one moved. One of the centurions stepped forward at last. He did not kneel.

"We cannot. You knelt to the Bloodletter before all of Solmiris. To save a foreign woman you courted behind the backs of your loyal citizens. We swore to follow an angel. A god. Not a man who bows to monsters."

Val-Theris said nothing. He did not rage. He did not defend himself.

He only knelt there, holding Jesenia within the cradle of his trembling wings. He understood—with a clarity sharper than any vision—that this was the moment his kingdom began to die.

"I wondered how long it would take," Val-Oros said pleasantly. "For them to see you for the weakened coward you really are." Val-Theris did not turn. "They always do," he continued, circling him. "The moment a god bleeds, the moment he kneels…loyalty rots." He stopped directly in front of him, forcing Val-Theris's gaze upward. Val-Oros laughed softly. He leaned in, close enough that his breath was warm. "I told you she would be your undoing."

He smiled when he said it—softly, almost fondly—as if he were recalling a childhood truth long proven.

Val-Theris turned. The world seemed to narrow to the space between them: bloodied stone beneath their feet, smoke thinning into a bruised sky, the distant cries of the wounded fading until there was only the sound of their breathing. His brother stood before him with blood on his hands and fire in his eyes.

Behind him, the *Hastati* stood rigid, watching not as soldiers awaiting command, but as witnesses to the fall of something sacred.

"She was never my weakness," Val-Theris said, his voice low, shaking despite his effort to steady it.

Val-Oros laughed. "Still lying to yourself in the name of nobility and mercy. How very *you*."

He moved then—fast, brutal, familiar. Steel rang as blades met, the impact shuddering up Val-Theris's arms. They had been trained by the same hand, shaped by the same god, and it showed in the way they circled each other, mirroring instincts older than memory.

The plaza seemed to fall away as they clashed, the world narrowing to muscle memory and reflex. Sparks flew where their blades struck, brief, violent stars against the smoke-darkened air. Each blow carried years of unspoken resentment, of diverging paths carved from the same origin.

Val-Theris forced distance between them and Jesenia, but his brother saw what he was trying to do and made every effort to close it once more. Val-Oros fought like flame—wild, consuming, laughing violently as he struck. Val-Theris fought like restraint finally broken.

Their boots slid on blood-slick stone. Shouts echoed around them, blurred and distant, as soldiers and civilians alike scattered from the wake of their fury. Their wings collided with a thunderous crack, feathers torn free and scattered across the ground like fallen banners. Val-Theris took a cut along his ribs and barely felt it.

His vision tunneled, prophecy screaming uselessly in the back of his skull. *Too late. Too late. Too late.*

Val-Theris roared then—a sound torn from somewhere deep and ruined—and drove forward with everything he had left. His blade found purchase beneath Val-Oros's guard, piercing through obsidian armor, through flesh, through the heart that had never learned mercy.

Val-Oros gasped.

The fire went out of his eyes.

For a moment, they stood frozen together—brother to brother, breath to breath—Val-Theris's blade buried deep, his hands slick with blood that looked far too much like his own. Prophecy flashed behind Val-Theris's eyes, this very moment predicted months ago finally come to haunt him.

Val-Oros sagged against his brother, laughing weakly. "You forget I have prophecy too, brother. Did you really think this was enough to stop what was coming for her?"

The words fell into his chest like ice. Val-Theris pulled back sharply, horror blooming too late. Val-Oros's smile only widened as his hand moved. Not toward him.

Toward *her*.

Jesenia had run to the edge of the causeway, her name already breaking from Val-Theris's throat.

Val-Oros turned with the last of his strength and plunged his blade into her. The motion was almost lazy. A final, spiteful act against his brother. He did not look at her face as he struck, but to Val-Theris—preserving the memory of the devastation he chose to leave behind.

The sound was small. Dull. Final.

Jesenia gasped once, startled, as if she hadn't understood what was happening until pain bloomed white-hot in her chest. She staggered back a step, hands trembling as they pressed uselessly against the wound. Blood spilled hot and dark between her fingers and over the small swell of her stomach. For a moment, she stayed standing, eyes wide with shock.

Val-Theris roared. The sound tore out of him, ripping through the smoke and the fire. Through the bodies and the banners and the stones. It was the final cry of a god watching his universe collapse on itself.

He crossed the distance in an instant, catching her as she fell, his knees hitting the stone hard enough to crack it. Blood poured through his fingers as he clutched her to him, wings folding around her without thought, without care for the world watching them break.

Her blood spilled across his golden armor, and horror flashed across his face when he realized he had seen this moment in prophecy too. The blade. The blood on the stones. Jesenia crying, whispering his name.

But he had foolishly seen it as his death, and was too sure of it to understand what he had truly seen.

"No—no, no, no," he whispered frantically, pressing his forehead to hers. "Stay with me. Please."

Her eyes found his, glassy and soft and impossibly calm. There was no fear there, only sorrow for him and what he would have to carry without her.

"It's all right," she breathed, though blood filled her mouth. "It's time for me to go home. Just let me go home."

Tears blinded him. His hands shook as he tried to stop what could not be stopped. He begged to the world, to the Light, to his father to save her.

Her gaze drifted, unfocused now, toward the sky she would never see again. The smoke parted just enough for her to see a sliver of stars. Her lips curled upward into a soft smile at the sight. Her hand fell. The light left her eyes.

Val-Theris made a sound then that was not a word, not a cry —something raw and animal and utterly unmade. He bent over her, wings wrapped tight, rocking as if he could somehow carry her back into breath by force of will alone.

Behind him, Val-Oros collapsed to the stone, laughter bubbling weakly from his throat as blood filled his lungs.

"*Finally.* A prophecy fulfilled," he whispered with his last breath. Then he was gone.

Val-Theris did not look at his brother's body.

He had seen this end a thousand times. This wasn't how it was meant to happen. He had always known his death was coming. He had prepared for it, accepted it, planned for it, even welcomed it.

But nowhere—*nowhere* in all the futures the Light had whispered into his mind had he seen this.

Val-Theris lowered his head slowly, his pale feathers stirring faintly around them as his jaw clenched, his breath uneven and sharp against the cold night air.

Something ancient and divine in his chest broke.

The Angel of Foresight, blessed and cursed with prophecy, had been blind where it mattered most.

THIRTY-TWO

Rohannes approached the room, but hesitated at the threshold, unsure whether to enter. The silence inside was suffocating. And there, on the floor beside the bed, was the king.

Val-Theris was kneeling, his wings spread wide around him like a broken canopy of gold and white. They trembled with each uneven breath. His hands clutched the edge of the bed where Jesenia lay, his forehead pressed against the cold sheets, his body shaking with sobs so deep they sounded like something being torn from his chest.

Rohannes had never seen him weep before.

Val-Theris didn't acknowledge him with words. He simply lifted his head just enough for Rohannes to see his face, and the sight nearly broke him. The Angel-King's eyes, once radiant, were bloodshot and hollow, his cheeks streaked with golden tears that glimmered faintly in the dim light.

"She's really gone," Val-Theris whispered. His voice cracked. "And our child—" He choked on the words, unable to finish.

Rohannes knelt beside him, the motion slow, reverent. "I know," he said. "I know, my king."

Val-Theris shook his head, hands trembling as he gripped the sheets again. "I saw every death but hers. What use is foresight if it cannot save the only life that mattered?" He bent forward again, his body wracked with sobs. "The Light made me to preserve life. To protect it. And all I do is destroy."

He wrapped an arm around Val-Theris's shoulders, steadying him, grounding him. "You didn't destroy her," he said softly. "You loved her."

Val-Theris turned his face toward him, a broken laugh escaping between sobs. "Then love is the cruelest thing the Light ever made."

VAL-THERIS SAT at her side for hours, motionless, hands clasped so tightly around her fingers that her nails had cut crescents into his skin. Her hand was cold now, light as silk. He couldn't bring himself to let go.

There had been no prophecy this time. No vision to prepare him.

No, that's not true. He had been shown it all, but had been blind to its meaning.

He bowed his head, his breath trembling as it left him. "You were supposed to live," he whispered. "You were supposed to outlast me."

A tremor worked its way through his body—too human for a god, too fragile for a king. His wings hung heavy, feathers dull with soot and ash, the radiant gold dimmed to the color of dying light.

He reached toward her stomach, the stillness there cutting

deeper than any blade. "And you, little one…" His voice broke. "You never even took your first breath."

He pressed his forehead to her abdomen, shaking. "I would have given you the world," he murmured. "You would have had her kindness. Her laughter. The way she believed in mercy even when it hurt." He paused, his voice cracking. "You would have been everything I could never be."

He lifted his head, tears streaking down his face—sparkling with a golden sheen, glinting faintly in the dim light. For the first time in his long life, his foresight offered no threads of fate, no whispers of the divine. Only the unbearable clarity of the present moment.

He brushed his thumb along Jesenia's lips. "You once told me you wanted as many children as your body would carry," he said softly. "And I told you I would give you as many as I could."

A small, strangled laugh escaped him. "You always did have a way of keeping all of your promises before I could keep any of mine." His hand slipped to her still fingers again, lacing through them. "I thought I was the one cursed by prophecy," he whispered. "But it was you who paid for it."

He leaned down one last time, pressing his lips to Jesenia's forehead, then to the place where their child had been.

"I will see you both again," he murmured. "In the place where even Light cannot reach. I will come for you, I promise."

EPILOGUE

The statue stood exactly where Val-Theris's vision had shown it would.

She rose from the ashes of the plaza, carved in marble so pale it caught every ember of the dying sun. Under his instruction, the sculptors had captured her face with aching precision, eyes gentle and steady, arms forever cradling a child that never drew breath.

Behind her, Solmiris burned.

The towers of gold and glass were blackened now, the air thick with the scent of smoke and melted stone. The great dome of the citadel had collapsed inward, the mural of his father buried beneath its own weight. The light that once defined the city flickered weakly against the horizon, too stubborn to die, too frail to live.

And Val-Theris watched it all without a sound.

He stood at the base of the statue, the ash swirling around his boots, his wings tattered and greyed. The crown was gone. The sword that once bore the light of dawn and defended the city lay half-buried in ash at his feet.

He had seen this moment the night before Jesenia arrived at his gates.

Back then, he had tried to change it. Back then, he had believed himself strong enough to defy fate.

Now, he only felt tired.

The city moaned under the weight of ruin, but he barely heard it. His eyes were fixed on the statue, on the familiar curve of her mouth, the delicate line of her hands. The sculptors had not known her the way he did, yet somehow they had captured her perfectly: that same quiet grace, that same stubborn hope.

He reached out, brushing his fingers against the marble. It was cold, as it had been in his vision. The same chill that had once burned through his palm when he'd first touched it in prophecy.

He almost laughed. The Light had given him truth after all.

"You were never meant to be a saint," he whispered. "Only human. Only kind. Only mine." His voice faltered, breaking on the last word.

The statue did not answer, and he hadn't expected it to. He lowered his hand, resting it against the base where her name was carved.

Jesenia of Lunareth, and beneath it, smaller: *The Mother of Mercy.*

He knelt there a long while, the ash settling over his shoulders like snow. For once, there were no visions pressing behind his eyes, no threads of fate whispering in the dark. Only the stillness of a world that had already ended.

"It was supposed to be me," he said softly. He looked toward the smoldering horizon, where the last of Solmiris's light bled into the clouds. "If I had known…if I had seen, I never would have led you to the very thing that took you from me." A tremor passed through him. "I am sorry, Jesenia."

He rose, slowly. The air trembled faintly as he spread what

remained of his wings. The gold had dulled to the color of ash, the feathers falling one by one into the dust at his feet. The wind caught them, scattering them through the ruins like fragments of a dying sun.

"I don't think the Light ever meant for me to learn love," he whispered. "Perhaps it knew I wouldn't survive it."

He turned his face to the sky. It was vast and empty—no visions, no divine warmth, no promise left.

And somewhere beyond the reach of light, beyond gods and prophecy, a woman's voice whispered his name.

Val-Theris closed his eyes.

"Find me quickly," he murmured. "Please."

A beam of blinding light fell from the heavens, and when it faded, only a scattering of feathers and the faint scent of sunfire remained—the remnants of an angel who had not fallen to darkness, but to something worse.

He had fallen to grief.

ACKNOWLEDGMENTS

To my mother and husband who hold me up even when I try to fall. I don't even know how many times I would have given up on myself if it weren't for you both.

To my personal assistant and best friend Samantha, who keeps everything running smoothly for me behind the scenes so that I can focus on the part I'm most passionate about, the writing. Thank you for taking the burden off my shoulders of constantly googling *'how to crop video on iPhone'*.

To my endlessly talented narrators, Lilly Drake and Sebastian Du Pont. I have an immense amount of respect for voice actors and am honored to have worked with you both on this project. Shoutout to the always phenomenal team at Blue Nose Audio and your patience with me even when I email you 100 times a week.

To Rilee Harris, who returned to give us the absolutely stunning and unforgettable artwork featured in the print copies of this book, and did the beautiful hardcover edition. You truly know how to bring my characters to life in a way no one else could.

To Shawn, who was my consult on the historical elements of this novel and was always willing to provide me with his insight. Who else would have a 30-page reference document on the history of Roman capes at the ready?

To my readers who make this all possible. Without your constant encouragement and support I would not be in this position. Everything about the life I'm currently living, I have you all to thank for it.

To my father, who is cheering me on from the afterlife, and to the American Foundation for Suicide Prevention, who continually helps me keep his memory alive. They recently inducted me into the North Star Society, and I am honored to represent your cause in this way. I will wear my pin with endless pride.

ALSO BY
ARIEL N. ANDERSON

Under Your Scars

Delilah: An Under Your Scars Novella

Venus

King of the Damned

Queen of the Wicked

Entombed

The End Unseen

and many more to come...

Instagram: @ariel.n.anderson